SEEKING MOTHER

India's Street Kids

Capturing Jasmina
Buying Samir
Seeking Mother

India's Street Kids: Book 3

Greenville, South Carolina

Library of Congress Cataloging-in Publication Data
Rae, Kimberly.
Seeking Mother / Kimberly Rae.
pages cm. — (India's street kids ; book 3)
Summary: "Jasmina wants to search for her parents, whom she believes to be trapped in domestic slavery, but she knows both the danger and the near impossibility of her mission"— Provided by publisher.
ISBN 978–1–62856–028–2 (perfect bound pbk. : alk. paper) — ISBN 978–1–62856–029–9 (ebook) [1. Human trafficking—Fiction. 2. Street children—Fiction. 3. Parents—Fiction. 4. Christian life—Fiction. 5. India—Fiction.] I. Title.
PZ7.R1231Se 2015
[Fic]—dc23

2015006940

Cover Photo: iStockphoto.com © pixelfusion3d

Design by Nathan Hutcheon
Page layout by Michael Boone

Greenville, South Carolina 29614
JourneyForth Books is a division of BJU Press.

Printed in the United States of America

ISBN 978-1-62856-028-2
eISBN978-1-62856-029-9

15 14 13 12 11 10 9 8 7 6 5 4 3 2 1

To Nancy Lohr
with thanks for loving this series,
making it better,
and getting it out to the world.

I will seek that which was lost,
and bring again that which was driven away,
and will bind up that which was broken.

Ezekiel 34:16

contents

Prologue

Betrayed. The word beat through me like the pulse of my heart.

This boy, nearly a man, whom I had wished so many times was my own brother, sat next to me on the pile of loose wooden planks. He kept his elbows on his knees and his eyes forward.

"Talk, Jasmina," he said, his words quiet but his tone steel. "If you value your life or your parents' lives, you will tell me everything."

I did not want to talk. I wanted to punch him with my clenched fists, to run to the house next door, bang on the screen, and demand my mother's freedom.

He looked at me and knew I would do his bidding. I had to.

My eyes dropped to the long, curved knife in his hands, a silent, cold threat that just minutes earlier had pressed against my neck. It hung loose in his grasp now, the fading sunlight from the small window glinting off the curve of the blade and slicing a line of light across his face.

"I trusted you," I whispered. My voice broke.

His hands tightened around the knife. If that weapon threatened only me, I would take the risk and fight. My mother's face, faded in my memory after so many years, kept me still. He knew I was his.

"Tell me everything," he repeated, "from the beginning."

"From when you came into my life with all your lies?" My stomach churned. I could not look at him anymore. It is little use to dig a well after the house has caught fire.

"Go back as far as you want." His mouth tipped. "We have hours to fill. Entertain me."

I fought the urge to cry. "Why don't you just take me to Gar and get it over with?"

"Can't."

"Why not?"

He almost smiled. "It's a secret, Jasmina. You'll have to wait. You might as well talk."

Despair flooded my body to the ends of my fingertips. I knew that hours of silence with him, there in the abandoned house near where my mother was a slave, would cause my fear and panic to erupt into action I would surely regret. I spoke. "I'll talk, but know that not one word is to entertain you."

He nodded, accepting my words, idly crossing his knife from hand to hand.

I looked out the low window into the darkening night. What should I tell him? Where would I start? My mind chased my memories into the past to the first time I saw him, that night behind the orphanage building . . .

One
Orphanage Rescue

My hair covered with a black and grey orna, my body cloaked in darkness, I slid my foot down toward the ground, hoping not to step on any loose gravel that would announce my presence. My heart banged against my chest like the knock of an impatient child.

I had not liked Grandmother's plan at all. "I need to concentrate on finding my parents," I had said. "Why can't the girl just go get her friend herself?"

"That would not be prudent," Grandmother answered me. "If she was caught, they'd have the right to keep her and even punish her. However, Jasmina, if you go and—God forbid—are caught, I can come tell them you are my house-helper and that you ran off."

I lifted an eyebrow. "Your house-helper?"

She grinned. "Well, you live in my house, and you help me make tea sometimes, don't you?"

I had to give her credit. She was the savviest old lady I knew.

"And, Jasmina," she added, looking at me kindly. "You know we could do nothing to find your parents tonight. Please help us do this."

By status alone I was bound to do her bidding. More than that, I felt truly grateful for her concern and help. She had guided my search in the quarries for Samir, back when finding my brother was my only priority, before I found out he was no longer a slave of the traffickers but had joined them. During my weeks with the white woman everyone on the compound affectionately called Grandmother, she had treated me as if I had value. Because of her grace and forgiveness, I had dared to believe in Jesus. Our evening Bible readings and talks were the happiest times I had ever known. How could I refuse her request to help someone else?

"I wish Amrita was doing this rescue," I admitted, looking down the street to where the orphanage building stood neglected and unkempt at a distance from the road, surrounded by barren ground as if a lonely orphan itself. Couldn't Amrita have chosen a less disturbing place for my first solo rescue? The hairs on my arms and neck were already standing on end, and I had not yet stepped a meter away from my elderly, white-haired guardian. My hand still gripped the canopy of the rickshaw.

"You know she wanted to and planned to," Grandmother reminded me, "but she could not ignore that call from her international liaison. Those escaped girls desperately needed a place to hide."

At that moment those girls were probably squeezed tight into the secret room of Amrita's salon or behind the secret panel in the sari shop nearby. My offer to do this rescue, or at least my acceptance when Amrita ordered me to come here tonight, would help those girls find freedom.

Amrita had said in her brusque way, "And you know once Asha returns, she'll not want you going on any more rescues." Her many bangles jangled as she gestured toward me. "Now is your chance to prove you can be trusted in dangerous situations."

Her words were fire on kerosene. If I showed I could be courageous and relied upon, perhaps my chosen sister Asha would allow me to continue working alongside Amrita, and I needed to work alongside her to set my parents free. I had to do this, and I had to succeed.

Grandmother waited patiently as I stood next to the rickshaw, considering the layout and thinking of the difficulties I might face. Once the orphan girl opened the window, I had only a little time to convince her to come with me. I could only pray to Grandmother's Jesus God—no, my own God now—that the girl would believe me and come away before we were all caught. How was I to convince her that the maid's job she was being offered was no job at all, but a sentence of slavery?

My parents had believed a similar lie and taken a similar offer. Where were they now? How could I even begin to search for them? My journal back on the compound was full of letters to Mother, questions without answers, hopes without fulfillment. The day I had filled the last page was the day I had stopped writing to her, hesitant to begin another journal for fear all those empty pages would have to be filled before I found her.

I had asked Asha, who took me in after my own escape, about domestic slavery before she left for America, and what she told me brought the kind of pain that comes when someone you love suffers and your body suffers in sympathy. Younger girls, like the one I was sent to rescue tonight, were more valued targets than people my parents' ages. The younger and stronger, the more likely they could be sold as slave maids or cooks or even brides to wealthy customers in the Arab countries, or to buyers among the small but powerful aristocratic class of India.

My father and mother, weary from years of labor to feed themselves and their children—back when Samir and I were still with them—would not have high value from a trafficker's viewpoint. That fact would not bode well for them, but would certainly have kept them inside the country and hopefully inside the city of Kolkata itself. They would have been sold to a buyer who could not afford a collection of young and strong workers.

In moments like these, I longed to write to Mother, to pour out my questions and my feelings. Instead I poured them out to God, silently as I stood there, giving Him my fears of never finding my parents or possibly finding them hurt or permanently injured and not being able to get them to freedom. They were not half the age of Grandmother, but any kind of slavery beat hard upon the body, even if their "master" was not the beating kind.

Though Grandmother had never been a slave, she was very old, and thinking of how her aged body near me could never flee on foot, if the need arose, brought my attention and my concern back to the present. I needed to remove myself from her first of all. As I stepped away, Grandmother's voice floated soft in the night air. "Be careful, dear. I will be here praying for you and her."

I forced my feet to tread slowly and softly across the gravel road toward the small field surrounding the orphanage building. A garden stretched out along the right side, several trash cans and even more mounds of trash to the left. I followed my instructions and chose the left side, though the other looked much more appealing.

The left side had been a wise choice, I realized. The mounds of trash housed several rodents and a few larger animals, so when I stumbled, a stray cat's frightened screeching made enough noise to cover the rest of my steps to the back of the building. Amrita was convinced the orphanage was selling children as slaves to houses or store owners once they aged out. Mandy, a girl of eighteen, had escaped to Amrita's beauty salon after running from the house where she was sent to work as a maid. The orphanage directors had promised her a job now that she was too old to legally remain at the orphanage, but after one day and night at the home, she ran away. I did not know the details, but I planned to find out once this rescue was over. I needed to learn everything I could about domestic slavery if I was to help my parents.

Though I could recognize the fingerprints of traffickers on even the basics of the girl's story, Amrita went far beyond supposition. "It's exactly the kind of scam my old madam used to oversee," she had told me, rubbing the bangles up and down her left forearm. "This is the lead I have been waiting for." She then pierced me with her black-lined eyes. "You have to go, Jasmina. If the woman who trafficked me is involved, I would be recognized. No one would recognize you."

My bravery was sufficient at the time. Amrita was supposed to accompany me and wait in the rickshaw, ready to assist if needed, while I sneaked around to the specified window to help Mandy's friend, who would also be eighteen soon, get away safely.

Now I wished I had stored up some of that courage, for I was on my own. Grandmother had a cell phone and could call for help, but if there were an emergency, a call to friends miles away would benefit little, if at all. I longed to be back on the missionary compound, kept safe like Milo, who could not move quickly enough with his crutch to be asked to do a rescue such as this. Or Dapika, who cowered even from the topic as if she were still trapped with her mother in a slave's locked room. Dapika's fear so paralyzed her, Amrita never wasted time asking anymore.

I took in a deep breath. I was the only one able to do this, so I should stop thinking and start doing. Focus. I eased my body slowly around the corner, then cautiously crept toward the second window, keeping low under the light spilling out from the inside.

I was almost there when something yanked me backwards, and a hand clamped hard against my mouth to silence my scream.

two
Grandmother's Gun

I struggled, but the person covering my mouth pinned me against the wall, an elbow and arm firm across my collarbone. I could not move my upper body at all, and weak kicks from my feet barely touched his legs. Another scream built up but had nowhere to go. I heard a low voice say, "What have you done with her? Where is she?"

Where was who? I would have asked had I been able to speak. At that moment, even breathing would have been good. I opened my eyes, which I had not realized were tightly clamped shut, and in the faint light from inside the building I saw his face. Before me was no man, but a boy. Older than me, but not by much. Perhaps sixteen or seventeen. His eyes were nearly black and his face hard as the stone I used to hammer. He shoved a little harder against me, and I whimpered.

"Where is she?" he asked again.

My terror had not muddled my brain as much as his anger muddled his, for he did not seem to notice I could not answer with his large hand covering the entire bottom half of my face. I started answering, and the muffled, disjointed sounds had the desired effect. Slowly, with a glare hotter than a summer day in Kolkata, he pulled his hand half an inch away from my face. I flexed my jaw and wondered how long this brute's handprint would leave a mark across my mouth.

Perhaps because he was the youngest trafficker I had ever seen, or perhaps because I just lost all sense, I suddenly found myself more angry than scared. I did not scream; it would not have served me well to be heard. Instead, I shoved my own hand over the boy's mouth to cover his groan the moment I simultaneously kicked him with one foot, scratched his arm, and bit his hand.

My moment of triumph was short lived. Stronger and bigger than me, he easily overpowered me again. He put his face close enough for me to notice his eyelashes were long. "Where is she?" He ground the words out. I got ready to spit in his face when his hand came up and hovered over my mouth. "Will you talk or will I have to . . . ?"

Breathing was important to me, so I said, "I'll talk." He lowered his hand and the anger surged again. "I'll talk," I repeated, "and I'll ask the questions. Who are you, and what do you want? What are you doing with the girls who supposedly get the jobs you offer? What kind of a horrible person exploits orphans?"

The black of his eyes seemed to fade a little as he regarded me. Why was he looking at me like that, like he just noticed I was a girl? "I thought you were the trafficker," he said.

"Me? Don't be ridiculous," I said, using one of Grandmother's favorite English phrases. He likely did not know any English, so using it would give me a measure of superiority, and I needed it. "If you're not a trafficker, what are you doing sneaking around here at night?"

"I live here, and I know you don't, so *I'll* do the asking. What are you doing sneaking around here at night?"

"I'm not telling you anything," I shot out. "How do I know you're not the guy who promises girls jobs and then sells them as slaves?"

His arm swung forward and pinned me against the wall again. "You do know something about Mandy," he said, his voice hard. "Where is she? What have you done with her?"

"Mandy?" That was the name of the girl who had escaped. How did he know her?

He must have felt how my confusion took the fight fully out of me. He removed his arm from my shoulders and ran a hand through his hair. I filled my lungs with air.

"Mandy is my sister," he said. His eyes swung to the side, behind, and to the other side. "She went to work at a house yesterday, but when I went to see her, to see if she liked her new job, they said she had run away and they wanted their money back if they didn't get a replacement in twenty-four hours. I thought maybe you worked for the directors and were here to get Sandy too."

Sandy. Mandy. Such strange foreign names. I stared hard at him. "How do I know—"

He glanced up at the window nearest us, above our heads and to the right, and must have seen something, for he suddenly turned and stood beside me against the wall, pulling us both down to crouch low over the ground. He looked up for several seconds before finally saying, "We don't have time for this. I don't know who you are or what you're doing here, but you have to stay here and keep quiet until I can get Sandy out. The directors are planning to sell her, and soon."

"I'm here to get Sandy," I whispered across to where he still crouched. "Your sister said—"

He moved, and I got pinned to the wall again. "Tell me right now who you are and exactly where my sister is."

"Put your hands up where I can see them, and get yourself off that girl this instant."

The command was stern, and Grandmother's face behind the boy was as sharp as the beak on a mother hen. My eyes widened. She held up her old, long, purple umbrella, the rounded bottom of its stick poking against the boy's neck like the barrel of a gun. He lifted his hands in surrender. "I just want to get my sister back," he said.

"Who is your sister?" she demanded. I told myself not to laugh as she poked him harder to get an answer.

"Mandy. I just want to find her."

"And who are you?"

"J. My name is J."

"What kind of name is that?" I blurted out.

Grandmother's umbrella dropped, and her voice returned to its grandmotherly tone. "Ah, yes. Your dear sister told me about you."

He turned his head at her words. Either the sight of an eighty-plus-year-old white woman, or the understanding that her weapon was not a gun but rather a scruffy old umbrella, knocked him back a step, mashing me against the wall. I pushed him away.

Grandmother's eyes narrowed. "So if you are the brother, why are you attacking this child instead of helping her?"

I wanted to get angry at her for calling me a child, but when she lifted the umbrella and pointed it toward him again, I had to slap both hands over my mouth to hide my laughter.

"This is not the time for—"

The light in the window above us went out. I found both the boy and Grandmother immediately on either side of me, all our backs against the wall. Like a clumsy, three-headed monster, we jostled a little as we inched to the right until the window was directly above my head. I hoped anyone looking out would only look left or right, not down.

A long creaking sound filled the air as the window opened. I held a hand to my racing heart when a voice floated down from above us. Soft. Frightened. Infused with the smallest hint of hope. "Mandy? Is that you?"

I nearly slumped to the ground in relief. It was not an orphanage director.

"Sandy?" The boy next to me whispered so quietly it seemed impossible she could have heard him, but she did.

"J?"

"It's me. We're here to get you out."

A little sound of something like joy came through the window. Then the girl herself climbed out. She did not ask questions when she saw Grandmother and me, and I wondered how many years of friendship it would take to achieve the level of trust she was giving this boy.

"Where's Mandy?" the girl asked once her feet were on the ground.

Grandmother answered. "She is safe." Her hand stretched out. "We will take you to safety too."

The girl looked to the boy—J—and when he nodded, she turned and slipped her hand into Grandmother's, as trusting as a child. Was she simple-minded, or was it just that she had not learned to distrust everyone like I had?

Grandmother and Sandy circled back around the building. I followed, walking softly, not scaring a cat or even a rodent this time. As we neared the rickshaw, I noticed the boy was still with us. "What are you doing?" I asked.

"Coming with you."

I scowled. "You can't come with us," I declared.

We had no idea if he really was who he said he was. He could be a spy.

A Fall

"Of course he can come with us," Grandmother said. "He needs to see his sister." She leaned toward me and whispered, "And we need his information about the orphanage to see if we can do something about the rest of the children trapped there."

My scowl remained. I knew my arguments would fall on purposefully deaf ears, but instead of closing my mouth I opened it and let something foolish come out. "But he can't ride with us. We won't all fit on a rickshaw unless we pile together and I'm not—" My face ignited when I realized I almost said out loud that I wasn't going to sit on his lap.

"My dear." Grandmother's shock emphasized the word *dear* into a three-syllable reprimand. "I had no intention of even suggesting such a thing." She gave a little huff, and then directed my attention to a second rickshaw I had not noticed. My face burned; I felt like an extended family of geckos climbed all over each other in my stomach.

The boy had the gall to grin. "Want to ride in the rickshaw with me?"

A little squeak of dismay was my response as I scrambled into Grandmother's rickshaw. He chuckled behind me and I pulled my chin as high in the air as was reasonable considering the situation. We rode away, three females scrunched together into one rickshaw, one aggravating boy with an entire rickshaw seat to himself behind us.

He should not have been enjoying himself, not so soon after the danger we had just experienced. He could have hurt me, pushing me against the wall like that, and should at least feel badly for frightening me half to death. By the time we reached the compound, I decided to simply avoid him until he left, and my stomach geckos calmed a little.

Though it was likely only seven or eight in the evening, it felt like the middle of the night. "Let's get you settled in the guest house where Mandy is also staying, and then we can have some supper and talk." Grandmother led the new girl toward the guest house. She seemed to hesitate until the door flew open and the escaped orphan, Mandy, came rushing out.

"You got her!" She ran to her friend and clasped her hands. "I was so worried!"

For some reason, this silly, girly exchange made me want to cry. I felt years older than them both. If I had known a friend growing up, would I have been as trusting and hopeful as they were? But how would I have known a friend? Had Father not sold me, he still would not have allowed me to attend school. "Teaching girls is a waste of time," he used to say to my mother. She silently bore the words, not telling him that she herself knew how to read, and that while he fished in the vast Indian Ocean, she had taught me. We pretended while he was home, both of us. We did our duty with vacant eyes, hiding the thoughts and stories that we guarded in our minds like secret treasures.

Remembering those days now, those moments when her glance would find mine and we would smile our private delight, I realized for the first time that my mother had been my one friend. Where was she now?

I turned my head away and noticed the boy with the strange name staring at me. His eyes were quizzical mixed with something that might be kindness. I hardened myself. Kindness was needed by the weak and helpless, by girls like the ones bouncing and laughing beside me or girls like Dapika who were afraid. Not by girls like me.

"I'll go prepare supper," I said with a rather abrupt departure toward Grandmother's house. The boy made me nervous, but I did not know why. As I walked away, I heard Mandy tell Grandmother that the orphan children all had jobs, and some were assigned to work in the quarry about a kilometer away. That was believable. When Samir and I were slaves in the quarry, quite a few of the children who worked there never came to the small shack to sleep at night. I never asked them where they stayed. No one had energy to spare for talking. And who wanted to make friends anyway? Any one of us might get sold the next day.

Was there a connection between these places—one that brought together the orphanage directors and the smooth quarry man or even the garment factory owner? What about the madam who trafficked Amrita? Was she a connection, and could any of this help me discover where my parents were slaves?

I knew Amrita would want to focus her efforts on the orphanage right away, and Grandmother would agree. Anytime word came of an escape, everything in the trafficking system shifted. Tightened. Children were sold away. If this orphanage really was handing children over to traffickers once they grew up, it would be no different. Time mattered. But my parents mattered too. Would finding them keep getting passed over for situations that felt more urgent?

I opened the front door to call everyone to supper and was surprised to see the boy standing at the top of the stairs.

"Jasmina."

The boy's voice sounded like Milo's, only lower. How did he learn my name? He took a step toward the door and me. "I will help you find your parents," he said.

I would not have been more surprised had he announced he was a butterfly in a former life. "What?"

"Your Grandmother told me you are trying to find your parents, as I was trying to find my sister. You helped keep my sister and Sandy away from slavery. I owe you for that."

My stomach fluttered again like a host of flies snuck in and were now trying to get out. I wished I could come up with some better image than flies or geckos when it came to my stomach. Thinking of bugs did not help me feel better. "How would you—"

I had not decided what else to say and had no opportunity to, for Grandmother, who had followed behind him, slipped on one of the stairs. As she fell to the ground below, I heard a painful crack.

A New Plan

Amrita's voice was sharp. "Your foreign missionary friends may not like the idea of involving young people, but I have no problem with it. It's a great plan, and I say we do it right away before the traffickers have time to create a plan of their own. It's already been too long. You know they have ways of getting their property back."

It was not polite, but I was purposefully eavesdropping on Grandmother and Amrita. That crack I had heard when Grandmother fell had been her hip breaking. I cringed every time I thought of the missionary doctors cutting into her skin and putting bone back where it should be. She had recovered well since then and could even walk a little with the use of a long stick to help keep her balance. Though my elderly friend still slept much more than she used to and needed to swallow special round pills for her pain several times during the day, that did not stop her from sending me to summon Amrita to her home for a meeting about the orphanage.

I had asked to come to the meeting, but Amrita said their talk might not be for "young ears." Had she forgotten I once lived on the streets? I needed to know if any of their talk would include planning to look for my parents again. Since her surgery, Grandmother had not mentioned my mother and father at all. I felt a growing concern that she had forgotten them, and even though she regularly told me I could ask about anything, I knew my mother would be horrified if I initiated a conversation with an adult on a subject so personal.

So instead of directly asking, I indirectly sneaked around Grandmother's house to get closer to the window where they were sitting so I could hear what they were saying. Rounding the corner, I nearly tripped over Milo's crutch. I righted myself, balking in embarrassment seeing Milo and Dapika, until I realized they were huddled under the windowsill right where I'd planned to be.

"Are you eavesdropping?" I whispered.

"No, of course not. We're spying." Milo grinned. "And don't look at us like that. You're doing the same thing."

I started a weak protest when J suddenly appeared behind me, followed by Mandy and Sandy. "It seems we were the last to get a great idea," he whispered, and I almost laughed. We huddled beneath the window while Amrita added creative embellishment to Grandmother's plan. I was excited to hear that I was in it, when suddenly everyone to the left and right of me scurried away, and I found myself looking up into Grandmother's face, wrinkled in amusement.

"You should have just knocked on the door, Jasmina." Her upside-down smile was dizzying, so I stood to face her. "Come on in," she said, then added, "The rest of you too."

We all piled sheepishly into the living room, and Grandmother introduced the newcomers to Amrita as elegantly as if we had come by special invitation, rather than via our detour under the windowsill. Amrita smirked a little, but mostly handled the moment with grace.

"You girls have English-sounding names," she remarked.

Mandy nodded. "All of us at the orphanage did. Westerners are more likely to sponsor kids whose names they can pronounce."

Grandmother turned to J. "But your name is not English."

He shrugged. "It was supposed to be. The director started to write my name on the birth certificate, but he got interrupted. By the time he returned, the paperwork had been stamped."

One corner of Grandmother's mouth quirked up. "The name suits you I think. Concise. No extra fluff." She turned to Mandy and Sandy. "Amrita works at a beauty salon deep in the city—the salon where you both are getting a job."

Their mouths dropped open, and J moved protectively in front of his sister. Envy clenched within me. What would it feel like to have a brother like that?

"Do not fear." Amrita stood, the edge of her glittering sari rising behind her like a royal cape of gold. "I am a rescuer. I do my job very well, for I lived many years as a trafficked woman and know the system thoroughly."

I turned to hide my smile. Amrita was known for beauty, intelligence and ingenuity, but not for humility.

"You're going to help us?" J looked at her, wary.

Amrita seemed pleased at his suspicion. Perhaps she got tired sometimes of men seeing only her beauty and dropping like dying goats all around her. "I am going to use their job offer to catch them in their own trap. You know they are already looking for all of you, and if their system is as corrupt as you say—and I believe it is—we will target the entire orphanage, all the way to the top. As they say, whoever owns the stick eventually owns the buffalo."

Her words brought the garment factory owner's face to my mind. Was he the *buffalo*, the man at the top she hoped to prod? Or was it the quarry man? Or Amrita's madam? I shook my head and focused again on Amrita.

"I know someone who is an expert on the legal aspects of these things," she said, and she looked at me. "He is with the same international organization that arrested the organ traffickers and the boy who was using your picture on Facebook. Fayeed, right?"

I nodded, swallowing, not wanting to remember how close I came to losing a kidney and possibly my life. On the couch nearby, Grandmother opened a small orange bottle, dropped one round pill onto her palm, and then carefully placed the pill into her mouth. She lifted a glass of water and swallowed it down. Was she in pain?

Amrita continued, "I will tell you no more, because you do not need to know. This man and his team can shut down that organization if we get him the right information. All I need to know is whether you are willing to help me do that."

J looked at Mandy. "I don't want you in danger," he said.

Mandy touched his arm. "J, think of the babies. They are so hungry, and no one holds them. To think they'll grow up and be sent to houses like the one I was sent to. . . ." She teared up. "J, it was such a terrible place. The house was pretty on the outside, and I thought it wouldn't be so bad working there, but once I stepped inside, they locked the door, and then sent me to the garage. They said I had to sleep on a mat in the garage with no light and use a chamber pot because the masters locked the door every night." She choked over her words. "If they hadn't let me out the next morning to empty the chamber pot, I'd still be there."

"I'll help you, Amrita." Sandy stepped forward. "Even if it only rescues one child."

Amrita had been watching me, but she turned and spoke to J. "If we don't stop them," she told J, "you will be safe, but their evil will continue. More and more children will be brought through their orphanage, neglected through childhood, and sold the day they age out. Can you really choose safety and security at that cost?"

J looked at Mandy again and nodded his permission. Again, envy sliced through me. Why had God given her a brother who cared for her and wanted to protect her, but had given me one who cared only for himself? Samir should be helping me right now. He should want to rescue our parents as much as I did. I sniffed and in my mind heard Samir ordering me to stop. It annoys him. I ran the back of my hand across my nose. Why was I still adapting my habits to his orders? I hadn't even seen him since the day I got rescued from the organ sellers. He was probably back with Gar and the other traffickers again. Why did I even care?

"Jasmina." Amrita marched into my thoughts as she had marched into the room earlier, speaking in that abrupt way that made her words sound sharp like pinpricks. "Do you think you could act oppressed?"

Five
Brave Warriors

Oppressed. That caught my attention. "Um . . ."

She looked at me, her gaze as sharp as her words. "You're quicker than that. Don't say um, like you're . . . oh, was that you being oppressed? Nicely done."

I stared at her. "Um . . ."

"Oh." Her voice turned weary. "You didn't catch on after all. Maybe I should find someone else. I thought you had more street sense to you than most."

"Goodness, Amrita, give the girl a chance." Grandmother entered our confusing conversation. Her hands shook in the way of aged people as she set out cups for tea while I tried to mentally catch up with Amrita. If I could not impress her today, I had little confidence she would prioritize helping me find my parents when this was over.

I had heard enough of their conversation to know Amrita was going to Mandy and J's orphanage this very day. She had already sent someone to contact them, stating she knew where Mandy and Sandy were to make sure the traffickers would meet with her. Now she was asking if I could look oppressed. Why not take Mandy and Sandy?

Milo and Dapika brought Grandmother snacks from the kitchen for tea time. I stood still, thinking, and things became clearer. If the orphanage directors captured Mandy and Sandy, Amrita would have nothing to work with. However, if she took me, and I looked *oppressed* as she said, then . . . they would see her as a madam, as a trafficker like them, and take her more seriously. Ah-hah!

Amrita was pouring tea into Grandmother's tiny china cup when I said, "Could you put makeup on my face to make it look like I've been beaten?"

Her eyes were now sharp with approval, and I felt a sense of pride. "I knew you had it in you," she said. "Let's get to work."

She stood, leaving her own steaming cup of tea. "I want to be there in plenty of time to get out before sunset. Darkness is playtime for evil people, and I want to be able to see all around me when I'm going in and out of that place. The message I sent said six o'clock. This being India, they will likely expect me at seven. We will arrive at five, if I can get you ready in time. This will give us the advantage of surprise, and hopefully get us there before any thugs they might have hired will arrive."

I stopped and stared. "Thugs?"

She smirked. "Don't worry. By the time I'm done with you, you'll look so horrible even the thugs will be intimidated by me."

Within the hour Amrita had me covered in several expertly arranged layers of paint. She led me to Grandmother's bedroom mirror and I gasped. The left side of my face looked as if I had been beaten raw. Around the red area that circled my eye was what appeared to be a massive bruise. The black and blue spread down my cheek and the side of my jaw, as if I'd been hit repeatedly by a hard fist or perhaps even a board or club.

"I look awful."

"You look fantastic." Amrita squeezed my shoulders, and I impressed her by wincing as if it hurt. "Keep that up and I may have to hire you to come on all my rescues."

My mouth spread into a smile, one that contorted the makeup into a grotesque pattern on my face.

"Don't smile!" Amrita barked. "You'll mess up all my work."

My lips dropped, but when Amrita added, "And on the way we will discuss finding your parents," I could not keep from smiling on the inside.

Milo, J, Dapika, and Grandmother were waiting in the main room. When we appeared, Dapika shrieked. I stepped back until I realized she was reacting to me. My face.

"Wow." J stared. "You look—"

"Scary," Milo offered with a grin. "It's great."

"Are you sure this is a good idea?" J continued looking at me, and I think his eyes held concern. "Those guys are ruthless, you know. They lock kids into dark rooms for days without food and water. They traffick people. This isn't a game."

"I know," I said, wishing he would be impressed like Milo instead of questioning my motives. "And we're all supposed to be there in fifteen minutes. You and Milo will be close by if there's a problem. So let's go already."

Grandmother settled us all down for a quiet prayer. As we rose to go, I was surprised to see Dapika step forward to join us. "I'm coming to help."

Had my jaw not been attached, it would have fallen from my face and dropped to the floor. I felt words wanting to come through my mouth, but they got stuck somewhere in my throat. Milo finally voiced my question. "Dapika? Are you sure?"

She smiled shyly and looked down, obviously uncomfortable with the attention. "I have been reading God's Holy Book, the Bible, and it says many times that I should not live in fear. It also says we should help those who cannot help themselves." She glanced up into our semicircle of shocked faces and focused on mine. “I want to please God, so I asked Amrita earlier to give me a part in the plan. I will go and help save those babies who need to be fed and loved.”

My mouth widened into a smile and I started to respond, but Amrita cut me off. “You can talk about religion later. We have to go.” She frowned at me. “And stop smiling.”

With that our small, untrained band of four children and one adult headed to face men who trafficked people for a living.

We were either brave warriors or complete fools.

A Tangled Braid

Milo and J rode in a rickshaw that followed us at a distance. Each time the rickshaw that carried me, Amrita, and Dapika, turned a corner, I looked back to see if theirs was still with us.

"Stop that," Amrita ordered after the third turn. "You're being obvious."

I swiveled back to face the road ahead, but felt my hands fidgeting in my lap like fish caught in a net. Dapika, next to me on the right, caught one of my hands. "Don't worry, Jasmina," she said. "God is with us."

"I'm finding it hard to recognize you, Dapika," Amrita said from my left. "I see the same beautiful young girl, but the words are from a different person."

"The Bible calls it being born again," Dapika responded with a smile. "God says the old is gone and everything becomes new."

Amrita's sigh surprised me. I looked to see her wrap her right hand around her left forearm, which was covered in bangles of red and gold. "I would wish to be made new," she said, so softly I barely heard the words. Dapika started to speak, but suddenly Amrita's face lost its softness, and she sat up straight, and her eyebrows arched high. "But I will never be under another's control again. Not even Jesus." Her left hand clenched into a fist. "Jasmina," she barked out, though I was still sitting right next to her. "Tell me everything I need to know about your parents. Eleanor Stephens—Grandmother—can't help find them now that she is injured, and so the task falls to me. She tried telling me about them but could not remember much."

That struck me as odd. Grandmother knew all the details of my story. "What did she tell you?"

"Just that your father was a fisherman, you had a younger brother, and your mother taught you to read."

My mind went back to my childhood to our one-room hut near the sea with its dirt floor and thatch roof and its smell of salt and fish. The feeling of hunger, not only for food but also for knowledge, and the curiosity I had that Mother encouraged and Father snuffed out every chance he could. Father was wind and I a small, fragile flame. Had he ever loved me? Was it foolish for me to want to be loved?

I thought of Samir, the brother who was pampered and idolized, the child who could do anything he wanted for he was not responsible for his own safety; I was. What simplicity filled our lives then, our exceptions to the everyday sameness a storm, a bit of gossip about a neighbor, or a surprisingly large catch of fish. Would I return to that simplicity if I could?

Amrita smacked my knee. "If you want to find your parents, speak. We'll be at the orphanage in five minutes."

The fish and bamboo and my mother's eyes left my mind, and instead I saw my father's hands, open and held out for money. "My father sold us, Samir and me, for a few hundred rupees," I said. "Samir told me once that Gar, the man who bought us, had set up a plan to traffic whole families. He had earlier sent someone to offer my father and mother a job being servants, but the job was only available to adults with no children. Then he came later and offered to take us children and give us free education."

"And your father believed the jackal?" Amrita gripped my knee, but this time it was to keep us all in the rickshaw as it swerved around a motor scooter driving the wrong way down the street.

What should I say? I was not sure. "I think he chose to believe it."

Amrita nodded, her face grim. "I see." She reached up with her hand, nails long and painted red, and touched the end of my hair. It had finally grown long enough to braid. "Your life, like mine, Jasmina, is a thick braid of lies and questions, of things we wish and things as they are. I have no desire to unwind yours and brush out the tangles, but I do need to know this. Do you truly want to find your parents and set them free? Do you want your life to be as it was?"

For a reason I could not define, I looked at Dapika. "Would you want your life as it was?" I asked her.

Dapika's eyes sparkled with sudden tears. "No. I love my mother, but the drugs took her mind away from me. Before, she always wanted me to be free from the red-light district, from her life, but after the drugs owned her, all she said and did, even when we were free, kept us both back there in that darkness." She wiped her eyes. "At first I went with my mother to the House of Hope. They slowly took away more and more of the drugs, and though her body was able to handle it, her mind was not." The rickshaw rounded another curve, and I felt her shudder against me as we leaned together. "She started accusing me of taking her drugs for myself. She—she attacked me." Dapika looked over at me with earnest eyes. "She didn't mean it. It wasn't really her. I know that." Her face dropped. "But everyone decided I needed to go away. I miss her, but no, I would not go back. At least this way there is hope that someday she will be well. Before, in that life, there was no hope at all."

For the first time, I asked myself what would happen to me if my parents were free. Would they try to go back to the same life as before, all of us pretending there had never been any selling or buying or slavery?

I had always been so fearful that they would not want me, I never considered what would happen if they did.

"I know you have much to think about." Amrita spoke near my ear. I realized the rickshaw had arrived and stopped, and noticed the orphanage building was much less foreboding in daylight. Even still, I had to force myself not to look back to see if Milo and J were somewhere in sight. "But you will need to place all those thoughts elsewhere for now. We are here, and I need you to pay attention and do the plan exactly. Can you do that?"

I took the questions, the fears, and the confusion, and as Amrita had said earlier, I braided them and tossed them behind my back, out of my face. I needed to think about them and would. But not now.

Amrita had stepped down from the rickshaw. Dapika stood beside her. "Are you ready to go, Jasmina?"

I closed my eyes to the image of the sea and opened them to the orphanage building. As Dapika had said, God wanted us to help the helpless. He wanted us to think of others more than ourselves.

"Yes," I said, touching a hand to my face to make sure the makeup was still in place. "I'm ready."

The Act

"I have connections on both sides of the system."

Amrita's voice was haughty, and I cowered away from it, whimpering a little. The men noticed, and I felt proud of my performance.

Two men were in the orphanage office with Amrita and me. One, a short man with a paunchy belly that hung over his pants, sat at a chipped wooden desk. The other was also short, but thin and wiry with greasy hair and an annoying tendency to continuously run his hands over it.

When we arrived, there were three men. At the sight of Amrita and then the sight of me, the third man quickly slipped from the room like an eel sliding into the river. I saw Amrita's face tighten. It bothered her that he left. Would he contact someone? The thugs she mentioned?

My job was easy, as long as I stayed focused. While she talked, I hunched. If she motioned toward me, I flinched away. To those men, I was a piece of Amrita's property, and she was making sure they knew she was to be taken seriously as a fellow trafficker.

So far it seemed to be working. The men protested when Amrita said Mandy and Sandy would be working in her salon. "No, we have hired them out as maids."

"I know." Amrita's smirk really was a thing to behold, especially when she raised her chin and eyebrows and looked down on the men. "But your methods of turning maids into slaves are pathetic. Such amateur tactics may work on your Western alliances, but they will not work on me. You are going to provide those two girls to me for at least two days a week—for free—or I will turn you in to my own contact, who will provide certain authorities information about the full workings of this orphanage." She leaned over the desk, and the paunchy man backed away a little. "And the officials I know are the kind you cannot bribe."

"What do you want?" The man's fingers fidgeted on the edge of the desk. Another scrap of wood chipped off.

"I told you already. Were you not listening?" She truly was intimidating. I wrapped my arms around myself and started rocking, as if the rising volume of her voice gave rise to my fear. "Stop it!" she shouted at me, and I froze, feeling a twinge of real fear that time.

"Those girls will work for me two days a week as payment for my . . . partnership with you."

"Why would we want to partner with you?" It was the first time the little one had spoken.

She froze him with an icy glare. "The real question is: are you prepared for the consequences if you don't?" With a quick turn of her hand, she reached into the folds of her sari and produced a cell phone. Flipping it open, she pushed one button, and then closed it. The sound of it snapping closed echoed like a slap in the room. I flinched.

The men looked at each other. I looked at Amrita. She was still glaring at the thin man, disdain all over her features. Then she started talking. She used words like knives, slinging them toward the men. A few frightening threats hit their mark. She said several things so entrenched in the corrupt system that I did not know what she was talking about, but from the men's faces I could tell they did. Then she clinched it. "The fact you seem to be missing, gentlemen, is that I have the girls. I can sell them today to buyers in Saudi Arabia for a massive amount of money, and you'll never see them again. I am being generous in my offer to only use them two days a week. If you want to see them again—ever—you will agree to my terms."

Less than thirty seconds had gone by since her summons when Dapika ran, literally, into the room. She was out of breath, and when she saw Amrita, she practically fell at her feet in deference. I would not tell anyone this, but I allowed myself to notice that Dapika was not nearly as good at acting her part as I was with mine. She was holding up a cell phone as if Amrita were the King of Phuket and she the lowly slave.

Amrita curved her head to look down on Dapika. She took the phone, pushed a button, and then held the device up to show the men. A video started playing. The men came closer to see Mandy and Sandy in Amrita's salon. The girls gushed about how much they liked it there, and thanked the orphanage directors for getting them such a great job. "You had the address wrong," Mandy said, sounding thoroughly ignorant and thus convincing. "And I thought you said we were going to work at a house. But this lady found us and said this was where you wanted us to work. We really like it. It's great!"

A push of a button and the video stopped. Amrita waited in the silence for a full minute, then said, "So you see, right now everything is fine, everyone is happy, and no one is going to jail." She handed the phone back to Dapika, who punched in several numbers, and then held it up again.

"I have your contact on the phone, Madam," Dapika said, her voice childish and afraid, her eyes down.

Amrita raised one eyebrow toward the men. "Should I tell him everything?"

Both men stood and started objecting. When Amrita casually waved Dapika away, and she ran from the room, I knew we had won. The men were nearly falling over one another as they agreed to let Amrita have Mandy and Sandy part time. I wanted to smile, and at the last second remembered that I was still supposed to be oppressed. I hunched over myself to hide my face and whispered a prayer of thanks to my Jesus God, who sets the captives free.

Captured

A whole pile of papers had to be tediously signed and stamped, though why a trafficker needed a paper from another trafficker was beyond my understanding. If you could not trust anything they said or did, why would you trust their signature on a paper?

As the stack of papers grew, I watched Amrita work her magic on the men. Once they agreed to her proposition, she turned all syrupy sweet. They seemed so relieved, and they started answering her questions about the orphanage without realizing they were sharing incriminating evidence. Of course they did not know that another phone was tucked into my orna or that it had been on this entire time, allowing Amrita's real contact to hear and record everything being said.

Finally the papers were stacked neatly and put into a manila envelope tinged with mold stains. Apparently the office was one area they did not force the orphans to clean.

"Now that I am certain of your generous cooperation . . ."

I almost choked. Where did she come up with this stuff?

"I feel secure enough in our situation to deliver the two girls to you, for now, with the understanding that they will be at my salon starting next week. Is that agreed?"

The men nodded. The round one's pudgy hands rubbed together. "Where are the girls?"

"Come with me."

Amrita ignored their continued questions and sauntered—she could saunter well—from the room, not even looking back to see if they were following. I stared in admiration until she snapped her fingers, and I jumped up. I rushed to catch up beside her and heard her faint whisper. "Are they coming?"

I looked back, as if as fearful of them as of her. They were half a hallway behind, but they were there. "Yes."

"This is it then. If this works, I'm using this method to take down and destroy the madam who once owned me."

The makeup on my face had dried and tugged my skin as we stepped from the building into the fading sunlight. Amrita stood several meters from the front door of the orphanage, waiting for the men, that haughty look back on her face. "My time is valuable, gentlemen." The way she said *gentleman* made it clear she thought of them as anything but.

The men did not apologize, but they did speed up. When they were near, Amrita turned and started walking toward the road. I looked around and sweat beaded up across my forehead. Dapika sat in plain view in an auto at the edge of the road. That third man, the one like an eel, sat next to her. Oh no. That wasn't part of the plan. Where were Milo and J?

My muscles began to tremble as we neared the auto. What would happen if—

Sudden sounds from the right warned that something was coming. Motorcycles. Several of them. Amrita grabbed my arm, and we broke into a run. The men did not lag behind this time. They passed us both in their scramble toward the auto. At the door, each fought to get in first. Dapika had evacuated the auto and was running who knows where, the eel man running after her. Amrita pushed at the open door of the auto, shrieking about letting her in and making room for her. The men tried to shove her away as the motorcycles circled and surrounded us all.

Men in uniforms were everywhere. They grabbed me, Dapika, Amrita, and the three men. One even got hold of the auto driver, who had much to say about his personal innocence.

I did not bother to struggle. Letting myself go limp, I submitted to my capture as if I really was the oppressed and owned girl I earlier pretended to be.

A Ride Home

Amrita was not one for quiet surrender. Her shrieks were like two pieces of tin roofing sliding against each other in a storm. She flailed her arms and kicked her legs and shouted all kinds of threats and accusations. The men acted in similar fashion, but since their voices were not as high-pitched, their arguments grated less on the senses.

Some kind of official vehicle drove up, and a man wearing a suit and dark sunglasses stepped out. His size was impressive and his bearing intimidating. He slammed the car door, catching everyone's attention and silencing even Amrita. I looked around. Dust from her kicking slowly floated back to its home on the ground. Behind the auto and across the road, far into the distance, I saw two young men on a rickshaw. It was too far to tell, but I think at least one of them had a phone up to his ear. I looked away quickly before anyone noticed my gaze.

"It's all over," the sunglass man said. He walked up to the three men. "Your orphanage is finished." Then he turned to Amrita and gave the smallest of smiles. "And it is a pleasure to finally have you contained."

"I'm not the containable type." Amrita kicked at him, a futile gesture since she was being held back by two strong men and Mr. Sunglasses was at least two leg lengths away.

He chuckled, and then his face went firm. "Take them all away."

Immediately we were all shuffled or dragged—depending on the level of resistance—to two cars with tinted windows. The three orphanage men got shoved into the back of one. Amrita, Dapika, and I were forced into the other.

Both cars pulled into the orphanage driveway to turn around, and then headed back in the direction they came. I noticed we traveled slowly, and the traffic filled in between our car and the other.

Next to me, Amrita rubbed dirt from her bracelet-clad arms. "I'm filthy," she said, brushing dust off her sari.

I laughed, and she looked at me. Dapika looked at me. I laughed harder, even though it made the caked makeup on my dry skin crinkle painfully.

Amrita grinned. "We did well, didn't we?"

A look in the rearview mirror from the man in the sunglasses preceded his comment. "Yes, you did very well. We've been investigating leads about this orphanage for quite some time, but did not have the concrete evidence we needed to arrest them. Thanks to your creativity just now, we have a full confession on record. They have incriminated themselves. In two days, we should have that orphanage shut down."

Amrita looked at the rearview mirror with a genuine smile. "So you aren't going to contain me after all?"

The man turned for just a moment to look back at Amrita. "I am no fool." His cheeks rounded around his grin. "Containing you would be trying to tame a wildcat."

His eyes were back on the road again, but I watched Amrita's face soften. If possible, for that moment, she was even more beautiful. Then she shook her head and her tone turned saucy. "If you're not going to arrest us, then I suggest you give these girls a ride home."

When Mr. Sunglasses dropped us off, taking one last lingering look at Amrita, she blushed. I could not tell if it was a real one or she had figured out how to fake that for some reason. I went straight to Grandmother's house.

"Asha? Is that you?"

I froze in the doorway. "No, Grandmother. It's Jasmina."

"Jasmina? Jasmina who?"

She sat up from where she had been lying on the couch, white curls leaping from her head in every direction. "I knew a Jasmina once," she said, pointing a finger at me. I stepped back, shocked at the gesture. Grandmother had lived in India over fifty years. She knew to point with her chin or her palm. Never with a finger.

"She was looking for her brother in the rock quarries."

"Yes, Grandmother. That is me."

She ignored me. "She went to rescue an orphan girl and met a boy with only a letter for a name."

"J. Yes. We just got back from the orphanage. They're going to shut it down. We succeeded, Grandmother." I heard myself speaking slowly, as if to a child. Grandmother lay back down, singing a song in English. What was wrong with her?

I heard Milo's voice outside. What should I do? I lifted a silent prayer to God and asked for help. If Grandmother was suffering from the sickness of the old, the sickness that affects the mind, I did not wish to shame her.

"Grandmother," I said softly, approaching the couch where she fallen asleep again. I had to protect her honor. "Grandmother, I—"

Milo's loud knocking on the door brought that swarm of flies back into my stomach. Why could he not do anything quietly? Grandmother opened her eyes and rubbed them. She sat up.

"Let me help you back to your room where you can rest," I said, picking up her pale yellow blanket.

"Thank you, Jasmina," she said. "I am exceedingly tired."

I clutched the blanket in both hands, while she leaned on my arm. "You know my name?"

She chuckled. "Of course I do, dear. And I also know that must be Milo at the door. Do invite him in. I've cooked a casserole for supper."

ten
Confusion

"You should have seen it!" Milo scraped his plate clean and asked for more. He had plopped down at the table and started dishing up a huge heap of casserole, not even bothering to ask what it was. He talked between large bites, running through the whole story again. "Everyone was running or yelling, and the men were grabbing people left and right. It was better than a street fight! If we had not known it was all planned, we'd have been calling for help for sure. Amrita was screaming like she was going to be beheaded. It was great!"

My gaze left Milo and found J. He, too, sat at the table, but had not reached for the food. A mushy casserole would be a rather large leap from the everyday curry and rice he would be used to.

I swallowed my bite of the American casserole but could not swallow my dread about Grandmother's changing state. From the moment Milo had knocked, she was herself again. Had I only imagined it?

"Tell me, Amrita," Grandmother said, her voice gentle as always though her hair was uncombed and her sari disheveled. "Will this rescue help you find Jasmina's parents?"

I sucked in a breath.

"Yes," Amrita answered. "Not directly, for I do not think the orphanage is connected on this level with the man who deceived Jasmina's parents into slavery, but I believe if we continue to climb this mountain to the top, we will find a snake nesting there."

"A snake?" I looked around the table. Milo continued to eat, but the rest of us had stopped and focused on Amrita. "I don't understand."

Amrita looked over at me, and I did not bother to hide that I was on the edge of my seat. "You know what we saw today, Jasmina. There's no way that orphanage was sustained by those two incompetent fools. Someone else, someone higher, is the supplier for that orphanage. We shut down one place of trafficking, but not the one who sourced it. What we did today did not harm the snake at the top, but it may have grabbed it by the tail. Whoever is really in charge will be angry. And he will want revenge. We can use that."

I shivered. "How?"

Her eyes swung toward J, who still had not taken a bite. "Him," she said simply.

Now I really did not understand. Milo spoke before I could. "I still wish you'd let me do it," he said around a mouthful. Dapika's face paled at his words, but he did not notice. "I already know kids on the streets and could get information fast. I'd find her brother and get the address in less than a week, guaranteed."

My brother? The address? I did not ask the deeper questions on my mind, but chose to start with a simple, unimportant one. "When did you make a plan?"

"I thought of it days ago," Amrita said. She put an arm on the table and as the movement shifted her bangles, I thought I saw a discoloration on her skin below them. She moved the bangles back together, covering her entire lower arm again. "But I just told J about it tonight while you were in the kitchen with Grandmother, readying . . . this." She dipped a Western-style spoon into the heap of casserole on her plate. Milo had dished Amrita's and been overenthusiastic. She lifted a spoonful, and then tipped the spoon and let the mush fall back onto the pile with a plopping sound that made Dapika giggle. "He has agreed to go into the city as an escaped orphan, pretending to give information about us away, while secretly organizing a way for us to find and capture that snake at the top."

The food in my mouth stuck to my tongue, making speech impossible. I could only argue with my head, and I shook it emphatically. "Too dan-ger-ous," I finally got out. "No."

"We already know where the so-called modeling agency is where Samir and Gar worked before," Amrita said. "J can start there, befriending Samir as a fellow trafficker and finding out where your parents are." She held her glass of water with her left hand and poured some over her right hand, washing her fingers over the plate of uneaten food. That habit, her doing it despite the fact that she had not used her hand to eat with, had not eaten anything at all, let me know she was not as confident about this scheme as she wanted to appear. I found myself shivering again, watching the water drain down the casserole and pool around it to the curved edges of the plate.

I had finally swallowed my bite. "You can't do this for me," I said, talking to J but only looking where his dark hands rested on the table. "Gar has a gun. He has no mercy." I did not say what I felt. *I'm not worth it. There has to be another way—one that puts only me in the danger. No one else.*

"It's not only for you," he said, his voice even lower than usual. "Along with information about your parents' whereabouts, I will also find out information about those who lead the trafficking in this city, particularly if there is a connection between Gar and Amrita's madam."

"Why would you do that?" I asked, my voice hoarse.

J, the boy with only a letter for a name, looked out the window and then toward the guest house. "My sister and the other orphans are at the House of Hope now. They feel safe, but I know it is a safety borne on the wings of a wish. I will not go join them, not until I learn who is the true leader of the orphanage, the one who would have sold them into slavery for his own greed. I will find that person and help Amrita's team bring him to justice. Only then will my sister and the others be truly safe."

"You make good speeches," said Milo, setting his spoon down on his empty plate. "But I still say I could get more information on my street."

"Your desire to help is appreciated," Grandmother said. She seemed to have just noticed her wrinkled sari and tried to adjust it, smoothing down the material with her hands. "But Milo, dear, these days everyone knows you live here on the compound with the missionaries. How long would it take before every street kid in the city was telling Gar who you really are to get a few extra rupees for their pockets?"

"She's right," Dapika inserted. God may have taken away her fear for herself, but it seemed much alive still for her best friend.

My similar fears for J were interrupted by Amrita's voice. "Your help will also be needed for this to work, Jasmina."

I put down my spoon. I would be unable to eat another bite, even if it were pani-puri soaked in honey. What did Amrita have planned?

And what would happen to Grandmother while I was gone?

Annihilation

J left that night. I wanted to wish him well, but of course I could not in front of everyone and was glad when Milo did for all of us. *God be merciful*, I prayed as the compound gate shut behind him. His task would be neither easy nor safe.

The next afternoon as the sun arched beyond its highest point, I rode an auto deep into Kolkata, where Amrita's salon nudged up against the worst part of the city.

"You're late." Amrita greeted my entrance with less enthusiasm than I'd hoped for. My stomach had been churning all morning, wondering what she had planned and how long we would be gone, and if Grandmother would be all right until I returned.

"Sorry. Grandmother was—"

"Never mind." She sauntered across the one-room shop and said, "Get a good look at the shop, and quickly. We need to leave."

I had only been inside the shop once and then only to hide behind the secret panel, waiting for nightfall and the opportunity to escape the organ traffickers without discovery.

That morning, I moved to stand in the center of the room and circled slowly, my eyes taking in information. I started with the front door, which was not really a door. The entire front opened to the street like most shops. A large metal closure was at present curled to rest above the shop, to be pulled down and clicked into place each night, locking the entire salon away from thieves. To my right stood one small desk with a calculator and pad of paper, for adding money I assumed. Farther right was one cracked mirror edged by a rusted frame that might have been gold-colored once. Two chairs held customers, and behind them, two Bengali women cut and styled their hair as they chatted. My eyes moved on to the back of the room, where a small door likely led to a storage closet. Next to that was a huge, floor-to-ceiling poster of a Bollywood movie star. Amrita was not the celebrity-loving type, but from its position, I knew it to be the cover hiding the sliding panel to the small room in front of the secret exit.

"Well?"

I finished my circle, taking in two more chairs and one more mirror. One chair was empty. The other held a woman whose hair was being dyed with henna, the henna goo staining the worker's hands a bright red as she rubbed it in. My gaze ended back toward the front where Amrita stood, her perfectly manicured nails on her hips, waiting for my assessment.

"It's not as fancy as I envisioned it to be."

She smirked. "There's not enough money to keep both myself and the salon looking beautiful." She turned and glided onto the sidewalk in front of the shop, looking back to say, "The salon can wait for beautification. I cannot."

I wanted to laugh but could tell she was serious. "O . . . kay."

Her hands went back to her hips. "Are you coming or not?"

I rushed from the store to her side. "I'm ready. Where are we going? What are we doing?"

"You ask too many questions," she said. "Information is dangerous. It is better to know as little as possible. Unless you're me."

She then moved her face closer, and I felt her look pin me to the ground. "All I want to know is, are you personally prepared to accept the consequences of your choice to be involved in this? There will be danger, and you must choose now whether you will face it. I won't have you backing out just when I need you."

"Yes," I said aloud, in case she mistook my nod for lack of surety. "Yes."

"Good." She turned and walked away, motioning me to follow. "Because today I am going to begin the annihilation of my worst enemy."

Wait. Annihilation? Was she going to kill someone? I had no desire to be part of anyone being killed. "Wha—what is your plan?"

She glanced back at me. "I told you the less you know the better. Now come on. I don't have time for you to stand there worrying. Today you're going to meet my old madam."

I stood like a wooden Hindu statue until she was at the edge of the next street. She never looked back, and I, finally gathering my senses, ran after her. She might just leave me in the middle of the city to fend for myself if I did not keep up.

Why did that strike such fear into my heart? I had lived on the streets before.

Once I had caught up to Amrita, I surveyed our surroundings. The streets where I had lived had been unpleasant at best, edged with sewage and piles of trash and overrun with beggars. These streets were worse in a vast and frightening way. Cracks ran up the concrete of the nearest building. I saw only one beggar, a hunched over man with a huge tumor stretching out his neck, as if he had swallowed a soccer ball. It forced his head up at an unnatural angle. I shuddered at the sight, even as my heart wrenched with pity. The pity turned to fear when the man approached two other men talking near the side of the road, men whose feet were covered in shoes rather than bare or wrapped in sandals. Businessmen. I had not been in this area for a day, but even I could sense that men on this street who were rich were not benefactors. I bit my lip as the beggar stretched his hand out, and then when he was ignored reached and touched one of the men's unstained shirts. Before he could even ask for baksheesh—alms—both businessmen had pulled knives from inside their clothing.

"No," I whispered.

Amrita glanced back and grabbed my arm. "Don't get involved," she said, almost dragging me away.

Had they hurt him? He was a helpless man. Had he once supported a family? Was he hungry? I had to look back and breathed out with relief to see him hurrying away, the two men chuckling as they repositioned their knives and one summoned a taxi.

"Why do they have to be cruel?" I blurted out as I stumbled behind Amrita. She walked confidently, as if she knew every step of the way over broken sidewalks and potholes big enough for a cow to settle comfortably in. One huge cow actually had, in the center of the road, somehow knowing it was considered a sacred animal and no one would dare move it so traffic could pass. Horns bleated like a complaining herd of goats as people and rickshaws and taxis and hand-pulled carts slowly eased around the cow.

With the advantage of walking and thus only taking up a small space, Amrita only had to shove a few people aside to get us through the loud and pulsating mass. "Some people enjoy being cruel," she said back toward me. I was surprised she had even heard my question, and even more surprised she bothered answering it. "For people like that, no amount of riches or success can equal the pleasure of hurting something."

"Or someone," I added. The cow—was there a different name if the cow was massive and had horns?—pulled itself to a standing position and lumbered out of the pothole in our direction. People all around us jostled, and I was shoved into Amrita and up against a wall of a shop. She reached up to brace her palms against the hard surface, and as she did so, her bangles dropped down her arms, and I saw scars, lines of scars long and thick. How had she gotten such brutal marks? She saw me staring, but we were packed in so tight against the wall she could not cover her arm.

"Yes," she agreed. "Or someone."

Behind the Stairs

While the cow wandered in circles, deciding which direction to go or perhaps just enjoying the chaos it caused, I gulped in air and tried to squirm free and dared another glance at Amrita's arm. I had thought her wearing bangles at all times was a sign of her vanity, not a shield over a secret.

The entire crowd around us swayed left and then right and finally broke apart when the cow chose to meander down the street farthest from us. Amrita quickly grabbed my arm. "Come on," she said, pulling me out of the sea of people. "Let's go before you get yanked away." She wrinkled her nose. "Or I start smelling like all these sweaty bodies."

"What happened to your arm?" I dared to ask.

She dropped her hand and walked ahead of me without answering. I rushed to keep up, my gaze taking in our environment as we crossed street after street, but always coming back to her bangle-hidden scars.

"It was the madam."

I was still behind her and could only see the back of her head held high as she spoke forward, her long, thick braid perfectly coiled at the nape of her neck with only a few hairs out of place despite all the rustling we'd just been through. Her pace quickened. "I tried to escape one too many times, and she whipped me."

I gasped. "That's horrible."

She uttered a sound of disgust. "No, the scars across my back are horrible. My arm only has a few scars from when I turned on her and fought back." At that she stopped and whirled around to face me. I froze at the black hatred in her eyes. "She wasn't expecting that. I took the whip from her and would have traded places, but she called for help, and I had only enough time to escape."

I could see her mind was far away on a memory, and she did not know that she grabbed my arm. Her grip tightened, and I winced. "Amrita."

She blinked, looked down at my arm, and let it go. I could feel the anger radiating from her. She took a step back and lifted her chin high again. "That is when I found Asha and her friends, and that is all you need to know."

"But I—"

"Be silent!" she hissed in a whisper that rooted me to my spot and brought my hand up to clamp against my lips. She had pulled me off the side of the street where we had weaved a path around the trash piles and large mud puddles from recent rains. I found myself under a flight of outdoor stairs connected to a rotting building someone had foolishly chosen to build of wood. I looked up to see a large board dangling right above my head, connected to the stairway by only one rusted, mangled nail. I started to step back out from under it, but Amrita's grasp on me was firm. "Do not speak, and do not move from this spot."

My head turned left and right. There was little to see and nothing of interest: several very mangy dogs picking through the trash, one street kid shoving the dogs away to get to a glass bottle that looked like it might still have some liquid in it, and one rickshaw with a driver currently sitting in the passenger seat smoking a cigarette. Across the way, a young girl squatted over a tin bowl, scrubbing it with a piece of soapy wet newspaper that created grey suds. "What is—"

"I said do not speak," Amrita repeated, looking around me to something behind. I turned as well, but all I could see were the descending stairs.

"Look through this crack." Amrita reached around me and pointed out two boards that had rotted away from each other, creating a slit small enough to see through but not large enough to be noticeable.

Glad to move away from the dangling board, I stepped forward and looked as I had been instructed.

"Do you see her?" Amrita whispered behind me.

I nodded, remembering not to speak. She was not what I had expected. The woman across the way who must be Amrita's madam was tall and dressed in an emerald green sari edged in gold embroidery. Her hair was silky and raven black, and it ran down her back in a thick braid like three snakes dancing in and around each other. Makeup covered her face and camouflaged her age, but she was not very old. In fact, her resemblance to Amrita was so strong it ran chills up and down my back. Their features themselves were not similar; it was the way they presented themselves. Even watching from this distance I could see the madam's high eyebrows and lifted chin, her gestures and the way she moved, all things I had seen before in the woman who trembled behind me. Yes, she trembled, though from rage or fear I could not tell.

"As you can see," Amrita whispered from behind me, "all I am, in everything I do, she is still there. She trained me, styled me, re-made me to become her."

"Why?" I had forgotten not to speak.

Amrita must have forgotten too. "To replace her." A shiver ran across my shoulders, but I was not sure whether it had come from me or Amrita. "I haven't seen her since the day I escaped."

"Since the whipping."

"Yes. Today I have to convince her I am not only beautiful enough to replace her, but crafty enough too. And cruel."

The shudder running across me now was definitely my own. "Will I be part of that?"

"No." She put a hand on my shoulder. "I'm not that cruel. She would see you and plan how to trick you into her grasp. No," she said again. "You will stay here and watch."

I looked through the stairs again. "Watch the madam?"

"Not her. I will be watching her. I need you to watch the perimeter, all that happens around us as we speak. She always has people out of sight, spying, ready to attack if there's a threat." She handed me her cell phone. "Call the third number if you see any danger. If I walk away from the madam safely, count to two hundred and then follow me at a distance."

I took the phone but nearly dropped it. I was shaking so hard I dared not touch the stairs in front of me, certain I would unwittingly rip a board from its place and ruin everything. "I can't do this."

Amrita did not respond. When I turned to repeat myself, I saw only empty shadows in the space where she had been. My head jerked around, my eyes swung back and forth. Where was she? Had she left me there?

I saw her cross the street and could not hold back the relieved gasp. Of course she would not walk out from behind the stairs and let whoever was spying know I would be watching from there.

She did not look my way even once as her feet, clad in jeweled sandals, glided toward the madam. She walked regal and confident, a force of angry, powerful beauty that drew the attention of everyone in the alley.

I held my breath, terrified the madam would bring out her whip. If she did, would I call the number and run to help, or would I disgrace myself by running away?

Followed

Amrita approached her former madam, an older mirror image of herself. Tension filled the area and spread until I felt it where I stood. Just a few steps from the woman, Amrita stopped, and the air seemed to stop all around her. Everyone near the madam and even people on the street stared, waiting. When the madam rose to her feet and opened her arms with a lipstick covered smile, the people around her laughed in that uncomfortable way adults do when they do not really think something is funny. Amrita smiled back, but from my vantage point they looked more like tigers baring their teeth than two friends reuniting, as I was certain the madam intended everyone to think.

Through their entire meeting, of which I could not hear one word, I did not run away or make any foolish sounds to give away my position, and I even discovered someone spying from a distance. I was not able to see much more than a shadow and what looked like a pair of pants, an insignificant clue since the person being a boy or man was to be expected already.

When their conversation ended, Amrita walked away, head still high, and I could see victory on her face. Anticipation ran through me, and the minutes were long as I waited to join her. What had they discussed? How was this part of Amrita's plan for annihilation? The madam stood and retreated inside the building just as I counted to one hundred and ninety-nine, and I knew it was safe to leave my hiding spot to retrace my steps back to wherever Amrita would be waiting for me. I tried to look natural as I walked out into the light and back out of the alleyway.

On the main street again, I saw Amrita's burgundy sari far ahead and smiled. My feet moved faster, and that is when I saw the girl. She stayed hidden in some kind of shadow or behind a market stall, but she was clearly following someone and that someone had to be Amrita.

I began to follow her. My movements did not need to be as careful as hers since she never looked behind her, something even I knew to do.

My feeling of superiority made me careless. I approached too close too soon and saw her shadow go very still and then disappear. I ran around the corner and looked down the street where she had fled, but saw nothing but another filthy dog and a beggar sleeping near a trash pile. My eyes narrowed. Had the girl been spying on us even before we got to the stairway?

"Are you lost?"

I jumped and whirled around to see a street kid—a boy—grinning at how he'd scared me. "Where did you come from?" I gasped.

He shrugged. "Around the corner. I saw you chase that girl. Did she steal from you?"

"No." The beggar woke up, and I backed away, suddenly fearful, but not knowing why.

"I'm surprised the madam let her walk so far away," the boy commented. "She usually doesn't let her slaves go anywhere."

I stopped. "She works for the madam?"

"If you want to call it that. Why do you care?"

I fought to keep my voice casual. "Do you know where the madam gets her slaves from?"

"Sure." He shrugged again. "But why should I tell you? You got some money?"

"No." I wanted to groan. Couldn't he just be helpful? "But . . ." I looked down over my clothing and finally held my arms out. "You can have my bangles."

"They're not much."

"Better than nothing," I countered, some of my old street skills coming back.

He crossed his arms. "Okay," he said, and then waited until I removed the bangles and handed them over. Once every bangle was off my arms and in his hands, he leaned toward me, and I could smell his bad breath. "She meets this really fat guy every Friday night just after dark."

Gar. I clasped my hands together. I must not show how important this information was to me, or he might demand more, and I had nothing else to give.

"One week the fat man brings girls to the madam, the next week he brings adults. Most of the adults are bent over and skinny. I don't know who would buy them!" He laughed, and it was not a happy sound.

I was gripping my hands together so tightly they went numb. "Where does he bring the adults?"

The kid named a street. "The fat man will meet her there tonight."

"How do you know all this?" The beggar was approaching, and my instincts told me to move. Beggars in general I did not fear, but I had learned to listen to that strange feeling inside when it said run. Grandmother called it a red flag from God. My red flag was up and waving. This man was dangerous.

"He supplies people to slavers all over the city." The boy shrugged yet again, as if his news was commonly known. He glanced at the man nearing us. "Why don't you come with me? We can take you to him now."

We? The other man came closer. The boy smiled and reached out to take my arm. I turned and ran, fast, not stopping even when I had left the alley and found my footing back on the original street. I rushed forward, searching frantically for Amrita. When I finally saw her, far in the distance and still walking away, I clutched my orna to my shoulder to keep it from falling and raced after her.

"Amrita!" I said once I reached her, breathless, "Someone—"

She turned with a hand to her forehead as I hunched over my knees, gulping in air. "Are you intending to make sure everyone on this street remembers us, Jasmina? Shrieking my name, running—" She grasped my chin and pulled it up to look me in the eye. "I would almost think you were working for her."

Fourteen

Pleading

I could not believe Amrita would think for one moment that I might be secretly working for the madam.

Her hand still on my chin swiveled back and forth as I shook my head. "No, Amrita, I'm sorry." I still heard gasping in my words. "Someone was following you. I got scared, and—"

Sharp eyes left mine and gazed behind me. "Is he gone?"

This time my head shook up and down like the Americans do when saying yes. "She. Yes. I was going to get close enough to see her face, but she heard me and ran, and then I went down the street after her. It was scary there, and I— I—"

"You got scared and panicked," she finished for me. I dropped my eyes in shame. "Well, at least she was gone before you told everyone in the area my name."

"I'm sorry, Amrita."

"Don't be sorry, and don't say my name anymore." The fear that had flashed across her face was gone. She turned and walked again, briskly. I followed close enough to hear, "We will have to be very careful next week. I know the madam will want to double-cross me."

"Next week?"

We passed a group of street kids playing cricket with a fraying empty cardboard box as ball and a stick as bat. One child hit the box into a puddle, and the pitcher ran to rescue the sodden mess. He lifted the box and murky brown water ran down the sides and dripped on his bare, dirty feet. He shook the box a few times, and then dropped it to the ground where it landed with a splat. "It's ruined!" he shouted. "You idiot!"

The pitcher barreled toward the young batter, who held the stick up as a defensive weapon. He was delivered just in time by another child yelling, "First one to find a new ball gets to pitch!" At that, all the others, including the pitcher, scrambled toward the nearest trash heap, pushing and shoving to dig through the pile. The batter wiped his forehead and sighed.

"Yes, one week from tonight, after it's dark." Amrita spoke again, and I realized I was lagging behind. I caught up as she said, "The timing at night doesn't sit well with me. She thinks I am weak, but I am no longer her slave." Amrita extended her left hand out from her side, palm facing the oncoming traffic, and we weaved a path across a busy street, skirting motorcycles and rickshaws, and waiting as cars and trucks passed. "She used to tell me that a cat in a cage turns into a lion." She adjusted her bangles. "She planned for me to become a lion in her service, but next week the lion will attack its former owner."

"My mother used to tell me that anger is a stone cast into a wasp's nest," I said, stepping over a large puddle and bumping into her to avoid a man driving a scooter on the sidewalk.

She made a noise that might have been a chuckle. "Your mother was smart."

I could not stop thinking of the word annihilation. "Amrita, are you going to . . ." I could not say the word kill. "Are you planning to harm the madam?"

She stopped walking, and I bumped into her again. "No." She sighed and stood still. I was glad for the respite. My legs had begun to ache at her pace. She sighed again and seemed to breathe out all her anger. "No, that is one thing I have learned from Asha's God. Returning evil for evil only continues the cycle. It never frees anyone." She held her hands out and folded her fingers into tight fists. "Though I have imagined wrapping these hands around her neck a thousand times, I will not kill her." Then she smiled at me. "But I can take away her position and possibly get her arrested, and that will make her suffer. I can enjoy that, can't I?"

I reached out. "Amrita, in the alley, I talked to a street boy. He sold me information. We don't have to wait until next week!"

She looked me over, and her eyes rested on my bare arms. "What information?"

"You were right." My breathing had finally returned to normal but my heart raced. "The madam and Gar are connected. He provides her with slaves."

"I know," Amrita said. "You gave up those bangles for nothing. He's bringing her some girls next week, and that's when we'll—"

"No, he's meeting the madam tonight," I interrupted. "Every other week he brings adults. I know the street name and the time. We have to go. If we can catch them both, one of them will have to tell us where my parents are!"

She shook her head. "No. That's too soon. We don't have time to prepare all the—"

"Amrita, please," I begged. I had to convince her. "Do you remember when we rode down that street on the way home from the orphanage, the street where Mandy was a slave?"

I had looked closely at the houses that day, but nothing about the neighborhood implied it was a place where slavery thrived. The houses looked the same as many others across the city. "How can you tell?"

"Tell what?" Amrita had asked, looking out her side.

"Which places have slaves and which don't?"

"You can't." She had rubbed her right temple. "It could be one house; it could be all the houses on a street. They might be small, large, fancy or poor-looking."

"Then how am I ever going to find my parents?"

With her fingers still massaging her temple, she had rested her head against the window. "Not from this direction, Jasmina. To find the people who bought your parents, we need to start at the top. With the person who sold them."

I had not forgotten those important words. "Do you remember Amrita?" I asked, continuing when she gave a slight nod. "It's like you said, if I'm ever going to find my parents, it has to be from the top. This is our chance!"

She frowned. I held my breath and waited for her to speak. She disappointed me by saying only, "I need to call someone."

Sayings and Sunglasses

We moved nearer a small dokan on the side of the road out of the main flow of people, and I looked at the small bags of shrimp-flavored chips for sale, while Amrita pushed buttons on her phone and then told someone that we were to meet the madam at the corner of—she said the very same road name the street boy had told me—just after sunset. When she closed the phone after another minute or two of conversation, I noticed something about her face had softened, and I smiled again and asked, "Was it the man with the sunglasses?" She blushed, and I grinned. "It was, wasn't it?"

The dokan man held several plastic trinkets in front of Amrita's face, and she waved his items away. "Of course it was. He is the liaison for the international group. Who else would I call?"

She marched off again and did not look back. "So we're going? Tonight?" I asked, my legs again complaining now that we were walking again. It felt like we had been on the streets for hours. That used to be my life, but living on the compound had made my body too familiar with comfort.

"If we can get everything worked out in time. I made a plan with the madam today, where I would supposedly trade a few of her slaves—whom I would free, of course—for information about girls who came to my salon complaining about their hard lives or an unwanted arranged marriage so she could target them."

I thought of my friend Kiya, who almost got sent to Europe as a slave. She had wanted to get away from an arranged marriage. I tripped, stubbing my toe on the hard concrete of the uneven sidewalk. "Ouch." I hopped a little for the next few steps. "But you wouldn't do that, would you?"

"Of course not. I'd planned give her leads that end nowhere."

"Why didn't you just plan to have her arrested?"

She tapped a long red fingernail on her chin. "Because working with her was really a means to an end. As with the orphanage directors, we are going for the man or woman at the top, not the ones actually on the street. I needed to get her to trust me and find out who supplies the girls and how." She smiled slyly. "As they say: if you live in the river, you should make friends with the crocodile."

Her eyebrows rose, and I was up to the unspoken challenge. "They also say a cobra will strike whether you call it Cobra or Mr. Cobra."

She laughed, something I had never heard from her, and I felt a moment of pride. "Well done, Jasmina," she said. "You're smart. And as uncomfortable as I am about the thought of doing something as early as tonight, I have to say that if what that street kid told you was true, you may have found the snake at the top for us."

I beamed.

"But I'll wait to believe that until I see it with my own eyes."

Her words were deflating, but I told myself she would be proud. Tonight would prove me right.

"Will I get to go tonight?"

"If you have the courage. I'll need you to watch the perimeter as you did today and keep your eyes open for clues while I confront the madam and hopefully Gar, if Gar really is meeting with her."

"I'll help," I said, "but I need to go back to the compound and check on Grandmother first." I wondered for the twentieth time how Grandmother was faring.

Amrita shook her head. "There's no time. He will pick us up as soon as we get back to the salon."

"Who?"

She continued talking but I was too worried about Grandmother to listen. We rounded the last corner toward her shop. I remembered that I belonged to Jesus now, and He could do anything, so I asked Him to keep Grandmother safe throughout the evening and into the night.

And us too.

Gar's Spies

Once, back in my bamboo hut by the sea, I woke in the middle of the night to the frightening feeling of something crawling up the skin of my arm. I jerked and brushed it away, and the next morning found a huge hairy spider clinging upside down to the thatched roof. I pointed it out to my mother, and then quickly wrapped my hand around a pile of thatch on the floor we were using to patch holes in the roof made by a hard storm. I swung the thatch high, smacking the spider just as I heard my mother say, "Jasmina, don't!"

The spider seemed to explode. Dozens of tiny black spiders burst from the large black spot and ran in every direction across the roof. More followed and more, over a hundred, many of them dropping from the ceiling to land on us. I screamed, my mother screamed, and we both ran from the hut slapping at our hair and clothes.

For weeks after that, every time the wind tickled the hairs on my arms, I started slapping at myself and flailing around.

That was exactly how I felt as Amrita and I stood in the darkness on the corner of that long-named street just as the sun set. The air was stale and humid with no wind, and I knew there were no spiders crawling up my flesh. Still my skin tingled unpleasantly, as if I would make a false move and, instead of killing one spider, would set a nest of a hundred free to fall on my head.

"I don't like this," I whispered. "Why didn't you tell Mr. Sunglasses to drive back here so we could wait in his car?"

"If the madam knew I had access to someone rich enough to own a car, she would know I did not need her partnership to traffick girls." Amrita did a full turn, looking all around the darkened street. "I don't like it either. If Gar doesn't show up tonight, I'm going to tell her to meet me at a different place next week."

Her uncertainty fed my fear. *God, keep us safe, please.*

"There. There she is."

"She's seen us," I said. "Maybe we should get out from under this streetlight so we can see her better and she can see us less."

"Good idea." Amrita's gaze did not move from the madam as we moved half a block to the side. The madam's eyes did not leave Amrita either, and when Amrita gestured to under the streetlamp, the madam nodded.

"She doesn't seem surprised at all that we're here," I whispered.

Amrita was unfazed. "You learn quickly to hide your thoughts in this business."

I looked down both sides of the street, watching for Gar even as I dreaded seeing him. Amrita watched the madam. My heart pounded, and I spoke to keep from thinking of running away. "When did she steal you away and make you a slave in the brothels?" I asked in a whisper. The madam stood at the edge of the far street, still far from earshot.

Amrita looked at me, and her eyes hid nothing. I saw the bitterness, the pain, the raging sorrow. "Younger than you," she said. And my eyes held the tears that hers would not.

"Don't cry for me," she said harshly, then closed her eyes and turned her head away. I heard her voice, softer now. "Just become what I cannot."

I took one step onto the empty street to stand between her and the madam and look into her face. There I saw the tears. She was younger than I had ever noticed. "Become what?"

Her eyes closed again, and she sighed. "Someone at peace. No . . . more than that." She opened her eyes and looked over my shoulder at the madam again. Her hand reached to cover the bangles on her left arm. "Someone free."

"How old were you when you became free?"

She clasped her arms and pulled them close to her chest, as if cold. "I am not free," she whispered, and in her voice I heard such lost hopes I longed to weep for her. "I will never be free."

I had started to speak when a movement on our side of the street caught my gaze. Had Gar arrived? What my eyes saw down the barely lit street registered only enough for me to reach my arms toward Amrita and push hard before the shot rang out.

Amrita did not scream as I did. She did not cry out at all. Her face paled to white, and she looked down, as I did, to the front of her sari where a circle of red, darker than the burgundy silk, began and spread. Blood spilled from it. Her face lifted, and she looked at me. "Jasmina."

When she fell, I screamed again. "Amrita!" I dropped to my knees. What should I do? "Don't die," I begged. "Please don't die."

Everything about her was still, and I was terrified she was dead until I saw a slight movement of her hand. She reached into the folds of her sari, and the moment her phone slipped into view, I snatched it up and frantically pushed buttons until I found the third number.

A male voice answered my call. "Are both Gar and the madam in sight?" it said.

"She's shot!" I yelled. I had forgotten about the madam completely. I looked up and around. There she was, still across the street, a satisfied smile on her face.

"Who is this?"

"Amrita's been shot!" I shouted at the phone. "I don't know what to do! You have to come right now!" My hands neared her blood-soaked sari, and then pulled away. "What should I do? I don't know what to do."

"Where was she shot?" The words on the phone were joined by heavy breaths, as if the man ran as he talked. Through the phone I heard the sound of a car engine starting.

"Right here, on the side of the street!"

"No." The voice was deep. "Where on her body was she shot?"

My hands hovered again. "Um . . . um . . ." I didn't know any words for that part of the body. "It's . . . it's her front . . . on the left side."

"Her heart?" The voice projected fear through the phone.

"I don't know!" I shouted again.

"You need the stop the blood."

I tasted my own fear.

"Use the end of her sari."

I reached for the long yard of material that had draped behind her in regal color, tears blurring my vision. My hands clumped it into a thick wad, and I pressed it to the wound. She flinched.

"Is she breathing?"

"I don't know." I heard a car in the distance. "Is that you? Are you coming?"

"Yes."

"She hasn't said a word. She's not moving." I heard myself crying. "Is she going to die?"

The sound of the car came closer. I turned and saw it far down the street. The madam saw it too. She looked at me, the phone, and the car again. With one last hateful look, the madam backed into an alleyway and disappeared.

I did not care. I forced myself to stay on my knees next to Amrita, pressing the sari against the wound as the car squealed to a stop right next to us. The driver jumped from the car and ran around it. Something in me noticed unnecessarily that he still wore his sunglasses even in the dark.

"Amrita," he breathed out. At his voice her eyes opened. I expected him to lift her into the car and drive us all away as fast as he could go to the hospital. He did not. He lifted her into his arms and pulled her close. She moaned, and I had to look away from the naked pain on his face.

He spoke to her, his words low and soft.

I did not hear. Someone else had caught the attention of my frantic, wandering gaze. It could not be. I would not believe the story my eyes told me.

My voice choked out one word. "Samir."

Taken

I stood as if possessed and ran toward the shape. He had retreated the moment I saw him, but not in time. I caught him as he turned the corner. "Was it you?" I screeched. "Following us? Spying on us?" It registered that he was faster than me and could have outrun me easily. Why had he stopped and let me reach him? "How could you?"

"It wasn't me. I was coming to warn you."

I did not believe one word from his mouth. "Liar!" I slapped him. The sound echoed and I felt the pain across my palm. "You murdered my friend!"

"Jasmina, I didn't—"

We both froze at the sound of voices, many of them, accompanied by shouts.

"You led them right to us," I whispered, my body going cold. "They were waiting until the international man came so you could get him." My heart thudded wildly in my chest. I turned from my brother and put all my might into my voice, hoping it would carry down the street to Sunglasses man. "They're coming for you. We have to go. Now!"

I started to run but stopped hard when the man holding Amrita lifted his face to me. Even from the distance I could see them. Tears. Streaming down his face.

That was the moment I knew Amrita must be dead.

I dropped to the ground—sat as if the world had stopped and nothing mattered anymore.

"Jasmina, get up." Samir was pulling my arm. I barely felt it. "Run. You have to go."

He yanked me until I was upright, but my legs would not seem to take me anywhere. I held my stomach and started sobbing. Samir pushed me, and I stumbled forward toward the car that I knew was too far away. The voices were close now, maybe five or ten of them.

"You can't let them catch you, Jasmina," Samir said. "Remember the picture Fayeed took of you and used on Facebook? They've all seen it. They all know your face. And whoever brings you to Gar gets a reward."

I looked in despair down the street to where the sunglass man gently but quickly set Amrita's body into the backseat of his car. He straightened and looked at me and at Samir behind me. I could not be sure because his eyes were covered, but it seemed his gaze darted to some hidden place on my right, and I saw him nod. Then he faced me again.

"Run, Jasmina," he said. "Run toward me."

Out of sheer obedience, I picked up my feet and ran. Away from the brother who might be a murderer. Forward toward escape.

Less than halfway there, from the right a figure shot out from an alley. I was captured from behind by strong hands. One pulled my left arm behind my back, forcing me into painful submission. The other hand held a large knife edged against the skin of my throat.

"Be very still," the voice behind me said.

Mr. Sunglasses had rounded the car and stood next to the driver's seat, the car door open and waiting for him. He did not look at me, but at the person behind me. Before I could get one word of plea past the sharp metal at my throat, he got in the car and drove away.

No! No. It could not have happened. He could not have left me there for Gar to have me. My mind could not move fast enough as the person with the knife pulled me back toward the dark alleyway. Amrita was gone. I was captured. I even thought of Grandmother being home alone all night. Would she worry I had not returned, or would she not even remember me at all?

How had everything gone so devastatingly wrong?

"Let her go." The familiar voice surprised me even more than the words.

"Samir!"

The person with the knife swerved around, and I by force went with him. Samir stood in front of us, holding out his own knife. The voice behind, which I became aware enough to recognize, laughed out loud. "You need a bigger knife, Samir," it said.

J? I almost said his name out loud, but his knife stopped me. What was happening? With Samir suddenly defending me and J suddenly holding me hostage, I feared I had lost all discernment of who was good and who was bad. The three of us took step by slow step toward the alley, step by slow step being covered by the darkness from the lightless side street. We were only a few meters in when the crowd of voices hit the main street and passed us by. I felt the body behind me let out a long breath.

The noise lessened some as the hunters spread out along the street. "They've got to be here somewhere," one voice said.

"I'm looking for that fancy international liaison. Handing him over to Gar is worth twice the reward for finding the girl."

My body shook, and the knife edge felt dangerously close to slicing my skin.

"Go out there, Samir." The voice had to be J's, and there was warning in it. Why was he doing this? He was supposed to be on my side. "Go tell them they had a car and got away. I know you want the reward, or maybe revenge, but I'm taking her in." For a split second, the large knife left my throat. "You know my knife is bigger, and you also know I am stronger and faster than you. Don't make me fight you."

Samir's voice found me in the darkness. "I told you once, Jasmina, that I would not sacrifice everything to save you." I heard his footsteps and then saw his face when he stepped back into the light of the main street.

Before he ran, before J pulled me farther back into the darkness, my brother said two words I had never heard him say. "I'm sorry."

Or perhaps I only imagined them.

eighteen
My Enemy or My Friend

"J, what are you doing?" The knife was no longer as close against my throat, but the grip on my left arm kept me from pulling away and running to safety. Despite knowing there was no place to run but back onto the street where men were looking for me, I still struggled until he gripped my arm to the point of pain.

"I told you to be still. We aren't far enough away yet for it to be safe to talk." He pulled me back several more steps. "Trust me, Jasmina. I'm here for you."

"Trust you?" I wanted to shout it but had enough sense to keep whispering. "You said you were taking me in for a big reward."

"I said I was *taking you in*. I didn't say where. Now be quiet for a minute."

A flicker of curiosity burned a small hole through my grief. "You knew Samir's name. Had you been working with him before? Was everything, even the orphanage rescue, all a big setup?"

He sighed behind me and dropped the knife. "I knew being quiet was too much to ask," he said. "If I let you go, will you come with me without talking for one minute? Then I will answer your questions."

I nodded but remembered it was dark as midnight in the alleyway where we stood. "Yes," I whispered.

"Come on then." He dropped my arm but then took my hand. The friendly, brotherly gesture was far more uncomfortable than the painful grip had been. I told myself he had to hold my hand to guide me in the darkness, and I clung tight, not wanting to be left alone with the reality that men all over the streets knew my face and that Gar wanted me found. I would wait for J's answers . . . and a little light to get my bearings before I tried to run away.

The silence as we ran was not good. In it I found my mind hearing Amrita's voice saying, *Become someone at peace. No, become free.* The darkness was not good. In it I saw the blood, the shock in Amrita's eyes, the tears running down the face of a man who must have loved her.

By the time we stopped, I was crying. Like rain on the sea, water on water, my tears added drops to the ocean of my grief. J led me into a small circle of light against an old concrete wall. The alleyway had narrowed until we could barely walk side by side. I looked up and saw that the light came from the moon, which until that point had been hidden by the buildings around us or their overhanging roofs.

After using his foot to clear some of the piled dirt from the ground beneath us, J dropped my hand and sat. He breathed heavily, as did I. My legs shook, and I sat too. A look around gave me no information of our location, nothing that would help me.

"Why did you do this, J?" I looked at his profile in the moonlight, the strength of his features, and the manly line of his jaw. "You only left yesterday. How could you already know Samir? And Gar's plan?"

My voice had faltered as I said my brother's name. As much as I had given up hope for Samir, to think of him as a murderer was more than I could bear. Tears formed and fell again.

"Please stop crying, Jasmina." I heard J say. I could not see his face any longer as he had it bent down near where his arms rested on his knees. "If you stop, I will tell you what you need to know."

I swallowed down my tears and hiccupped—such a foolish, involuntary motion that should not happen alongside grief. The reason I grieved burned deep inside me and more hot tears came, but I forced them away, biting my lips and focusing on the pain to keep still and silent.

J lifted his head and looked at me. "None of this should have happened tonight. I'm sorry about your friend."

My teeth bit harder. I tasted blood on my lip. "How did you know about tonight?"

"Gar. He told all of us—the men who work for him—to come to this street at a certain time and capture you, Amrita, and the international liaison. Gar passed your picture around, Jasmina. I nearly lost my cover when I saw it. I almost said your name." He looked me in the eye. "Do you have any idea how much danger you are in? That man is thick with evil."

I wrapped my arms around myself. "I don't understand. How did he know—"

He interrupted me. "If I had found out sooner, I would have warned you and Amrita both. After Gar dismissed the others, he told Samir and me that we should come directly here, and whichever of us got to you first got the reward. It was a test for Samir's loyalty. From the moment I found them, Gar has been using me as competition for Samir, to get him to do things to prove himself."

"How did you find them so quickly?" The muscles in my arms ached from clenching them so tightly.

"Finding them was not hard. Amrita had told me where the modeling agency was where you and some other girls had been taken. A few mentions to guys on the street that I had information about the orphanage rescue, and, before the night was over, Gar found me. I fed him just enough to be believable, and all day today he has been testing me as well as Samir. He said he had a big plan that would put him far ahead of the other traffickers. I had no idea he was talking about Amrita and the international connection. The moment Gar told us to go right away, I ran. I called the connection."

"Don't you know his name either?"

J shook his head. "No one does. I called him and told him everything. We were trying to make a plan to get you both out when your call came through. He hung up on me, and I ran the rest of the way there. I had just arrived when Samir was telling you to get up."

"But how did Gar know?"

"We were foolish." J put his head down into his hands. "Foolish to think they were not all connected. Amrita was not the only person followed today. You were as well."

My arms would not hold out any longer. They dropped to my sides, quivering. "Me? Why?"

"You made a fool of Gar, and he wants revenge. Amrita's madam really does get her supply of new slaves through him, and—"

"He's the snake at the top," I whispered. Would this man strike every person I loved?

"Amrita's plan made the madam suspicious, so she had Amrita followed."

"I know." My lip continued to bleed. I wiped at it. "I discovered her."

"And someone discovered you. That street kid you met, whoever he was, recognized your picture from when Fayeed used it at the modeling agency. He ran to Gar. Once Gar knew you were connected with Amrita, there was no hope for any of this to succeed."

No amount of biting my lip could keep the tears away. "So it's my fault." I choked on a sob. "She's dead, and it's my fault."

"Jasmina . . ."

I did not look at him, wondering what he could possibly say. How could we all have been so blind? We had walked into a field of high grass, foolish enough to believe no predators lay hidden there.

"The only thing good about all of this is that I know now where your father is."

I glanced over at him through my tears. "How—"

"When Fayeed got arrested, Samir decided to take over his position, but Gar tried to keep him in place by threatening your parents. He told Samir that your father had tried to escape, and so he sent your father to the worst brick kiln in the city as punishment. Samir was so mad, it didn't take much to get him to tell me which one. I'm starting to think your brother wishes he could get out of it all, Jasmina. I think he really did come to warn you tonight."

Grief crashed on me in another wave. I finally had information about one of my parents, but at what cost? And even if we did find my father, how could I tell him why the one searching for him was not his beloved son?

J reached down and took my trembling hand in his own. As if reading my mind, recognizing that the touch would only be customary were he a relation, he said, "Tonight, I will be your brother."

My voice caught. "My brother is a trafficker. Maybe a murderer."

He sighed, and his voice was as soft as the moonlight around us. "Then tonight I will be your friend."

Going Back

We sat silent for long minutes, and I took comfort having my hand in J's. So much of me felt lost and alone, just having that one small part of me wrapped inside the strength of his hand eased some of the pain.

There were still details I did not understand and questions I had not asked, but knowing I had a friend there in the darkness was enough for that moment. When J stood and helped me to my feet, I rose reluctantly, knowing I would end this journey alone.

"I have to go back to them," he said, leading me farther down the alleyway and back into darkness.

"It's not safe."

"I know." He still held my hand in his. "But if I don't finish this, Amrita got shot for nothing, and I will not let that happen. I still need to find out where your mother is. Jasmina, we will find your parents, set them free, and take you all away where you will be safe."

My head was shaking back and forth before he finished talking. "No, J, you need to come back with me now." I squeezed his hand tight as we walked, adding urgency to my words. "If they discovered my connection with Amrita and the international liaison, how do you know they don't already know about yours? What if they are trapping you?"

He ignored my question, saying instead, "I shouldn't go any farther." We had stopped one block away from a lit street. "I'm going back the way we came," he said. "Samir doesn't know the address where your mother is a slave. Gar said he moved her recently to keep Samir under his control. I will go back and gain Gar's trust and get that address. Hopefully, you will hear from me soon."

"How can you gain Gar's trust? J, don't do this." I heard the fear in my voice—fear for him.

"Gaining his trust will be easy. I'm going to rush to him tonight very angry because a certain young woman escaped me, despite my overpowering size and strength." He surprised me with his smile and the joke; he was taller than me by barely an inch. "I will tell Gar I plan to capture you at any cost, and since he wants revenge, he will gladly help me."

How could he smile? "I don't feel good about any of this."

"It's what we have to do." He looked down at me. "You need to go now. Stay in the shadows whenever you can. I will find a way to contact you when I have news."

His thumb rubbed across the top of my hand before he let it go.

"But how will I know how to get back?" I asked, looking through the semi-darkness to the light beyond. "I don't even know where we are."

J did not answer. I turned to ask again, but no friend stood beside me. Only a slight brush of air touched me from where he had stood. I heard the running pad of his footsteps and wanted to call out to him. Instead, my tongue brushed across the sore section of my lip, and I faced the street ahead and moved toward the light.

When I reached the street, I remained in the safe cave my alleyway provided and took a look around. There, across the road and to the right, was Amrita's salon. I wanted to cry again. J knew I could get back to the compound from there. He had not left me to wander alone in an unknown place.

Hedging around corners and under awnings, I kept off the main part of the street as long as possible. Once my path was directly across from Amrita's salon, I let the fear make my feet wings. I dashed across the street, around the block that housed her shop, and found the narrow path behind it. That path would take me home.

I ran the entire way, my lungs burning, my heart pumping my fear and anger through my body. The lights of the compound welcomed me, and I forgot the pain in my feet and the pain in my heart. I sprinted to the gate and flattened my palm against it, creating sounds of thunder as I pounded against the metal.

The gate opened a crack. Milo's father looked me over, and his eyes went wide. He pulled the gate open, and I rushed inside, again running as if Gar himself chased me, which he never would. His huge girth would keep him slow, so he would have his coolies pursue me instead, as they had already that night.

Memories of the greed in their voices, the delightful prospect of a reward in exchange for a person, pushed all other thoughts from my mind. I ran straight through the middle of the compound, leaping over plants in the missionaries' garden, swerving around bushes, my eyes fastened on my destination.

"Jasmina, you're finally back! Did you know that—"

I heard Dapika's voice calling to me from the orphanage building, but I did not stop. I did not even turn. I continued toward Grandmother's house. I hoped she was asleep. I hoped the house would be dark and silent and I could go into her guest room with the cheerful yellow blanket draped across the bed. I wanted to bury my face into its softness and cry and cry until all the tears were gone.

As I neared the house, I could see that the light outside, the light she left on for me when I was out, was not the only one shining through the darkness. At least one more light was on inside.

I considered running around the house and hiding under Grandmother's large bushes, digging myself a hole where I could hide unnoticed, like the house key she kept buried there in case she locked herself out. But Grandmother was surely already worried about me. That was probably why she had not gone to sleep. I should not make her suffer.

I burst through the door yelling, "Grandmother!" and stopped so quickly I nearly fell.

How many impossible surprises would I face tonight?

There, in the room right in front of me near where Grandmother sat on the couch holding baby Adiya, stood Asha and Mr. Mark. My chosen family. The family that was supposed to still be in America.

Asha opened her arms just as the madam had to Amrita, except her smile was genuine. "Jasmina! I'm so happy—"

Her eyes dropped to my clothes, and suddenly we all spoke at once.

"What are you doing here?" was all I could think to ask.

"Didn't Grams tell you we were coming back today?" Those words came from Mr. Mark.

"Me?" Grandmother frowned at me. "Why would I tell her? Who is she?"

I groaned. Mr. Mark's frown went lower. Baby Adiya squealed.

Asha stopped us all with her gasping question. "Jasmina, you're covered in blood. What on earth happened to you?"

I looked down and saw my clothes, the dark red stains from blood already dried up and lifeless. I choked out the words, "Amrita, she's—she got shot! Her heart. She's—she's—"

That time, when Asha's arms went out again, I rushed into them, weeping.

Grief

Mr. Mark helped Grandmother to bed. I knew he and Asha would want to know more about her and why she did not remember me, but that could wait an hour or so. Grandmother had handed baby Adiya back to Asha and chattered happily to Mr. Mark, pill bottle in hand, as they left the room. Asha then quietly suggested I go change my clothes while she got the baby ready for bed, and then we could talk.

I did not at first think I would have anything to say. I changed into a clean shalwar kameez and put the one covered in blood into the trash can under the kitchen sink. I never wanted my eyes to look upon it again. A glance down at my hands showed they, too, bore the stains of death. I went back to the guest room, the place that had been my home for weeks, such a safe place, and removed the clean outfit so I could douse my entire body with water and scrub myself free of at least the color of the violence I had seen. I watched red flow with the water down toward the drain and away. Would that I could as easily wash away the sights and smells that stained my memories.

By the time I emerged, Asha sat waiting for me on the couch in the main room. I could hear baby Adiya cooing happily in the room down the hall, and from another room I heard Grandmother telling Mr. Mark about the orphanage rescue, her voice filled with pride and girlish excitement.

"Let's go sit outside for a while, shall we?" Asha stood and held out her hand, and like a small child I took it and followed her. From my bare toes up through my middle and even to my mind, I felt numb.

We walked around the house and outside to the very bush I had longed to hide under earlier. Behind the bush, Asha sat cross-legged on the ground and motioned for me to sit next to her. From there the bush blocked the lights from the compound houses and made it possible to see many stars. I thought of my childhood home near the sea, of how the sky became beautiful at night, a shawl of darkness jeweled all over with stars, and wondered if I would ever see my mother again.

Asha did not ask for information from me, and I did not ask for any from her. Had she arrived the night before, I would have poured questions upon her about America and her family and so many other things I had wanted to know that now seemed unimportant. My information, my experience that night, was very important, yet she did not ask. We sat in silence until I found myself speaking. I kept my head tilted up and spoke toward the stars. It spilled from me, the story, the madam, J, Samir, my father being sent to a brick kiln, Amrita's face when the bullet entered her body. I told Asha everything, and, without looking at her, I sensed she was crying.

When I stopped, the words gone leaving me empty as if my soul had poured out with them, she still did not speak. I looked over to see her, face upward, her mouth moving and tears running down her cheeks. She was praying.

I had not thought to pray. Not once since that prayer I had uttered before the gunshot when I had asked God to keep us safe. Had God not heard me? Had He chosen only to keep me safe and not Amrita, since she refused to become His child?

What was Amrita's fate now? *I will never be free*, she had said. I lowered my head and cried again. Was there no end to my tears?

"Look up, Jasmina," Asha's gentle voice said. "Look at the sky. The heavens declare the glory of God."

She often said strange things. I was surprised she had not jumped up to call the international connection or make a plan or do something. I looked up as she'd told me to and saw above me thousands of lights, tiny and so far away.

"I remember when I lived in a village in Bangladesh for a while," Asha said, her face still bent back to look upward. "At night I would go outside and spend hours looking up. I had never seen such a sight."

I glanced her way. "You do not have stars in America?"

Her mouth curved into a small, sad smile. "We do. But there are always lights on at night—in the homes and the buildings—and it makes the stars harder to see. I had no idea so many stars even existed." She looked at me and touched a soft hand to my hair. "Did you know that the Bible says God numbers the stars and knows them all by name?"

Grandmother must have told Asha during a moment when she remembered me that I had become a follower of Jesus while they were in America. Or perhaps she hadn't. Asha talked of her God as easily as she breathed. I had much to tell her from her time away. But not tonight. "The stars have names?" I looked up again. So many thousands. "Why?"

"I don't know," Asha said. "But I love how it tells me that God enjoys His creation and knows all about it. If He even has a name for every one of the millions of stars, I know that I'm not too small or unimportant for Him to pay attention to me. He is the God of the wondrous and amazing galaxies, but also the God who puts incredible details into every leaf on a tree and each tiny little ant." She sighed, and I sighed with her. "Amazing," she said, "that we would matter to Him at all."

Her hand touched my hair again, the touch of a mother. "Jasmina, I'm so sorry for what you saw and experienced tonight. I am very grieved for Amrita. I do not understand what happened or why, but I do know this." She turned to look me full in the face. "God knows you. He loves you. And He does have a way to make this work for good." Her eyes overflowed. "Though I admit I cannot right now see how."

She stood, but I remained as rooted to my spot as the bush behind me. "Stay as long as you need to, Jasmina," she told me, her voice kind. "I'll leave the door unlocked and the front light on."

My chosen sister went inside, but I remained outside for some time, looking up into the sky, wondering about the God who knew all the stars by name.

Pills and Questions

Light slid through my open window the next morning. The sun had still come up. The day had still arrived. I did not want it to. I wanted to sleep, to forget, to reject the simple everyday exercises of washing and getting dressed. It should not be an everyday kind of day. Tragedy had touched me, and life should exempt me from all such expectations. How was I to rise, to eat and drink, to brush my teeth, as if something terrible had not happened to shred my heart with the promise of more terrible things coming?

I needed to tell Asha and Mr. Mark about the danger I was in, a danger I may have spread to everyone on the compound by my mere presence.

Love for them told me I should leave to protect their safety. But I needed their help to rescue my father.

I had no idea what to do.

With heavy steps, unaware of what I wore and not caring if I had even brushed my hair, I left my room and encountered Grandmother in the hallway. "Jasmina!" She greeted me with a tight hug. "I had the worst dream about you last night and have been praying for you all morning. I kept wanting to go into your room to check to see if you'd gotten home safely, but I did not want to wake you. You must have arrived home after I fell asleep. I'm so glad you are safe and back with us."

Mr. Mark must have heard her voice—he certainly did not hear my dumbfounded silence—and came to escort us both to the table where Asha had already prepared an American breakfast of eggs, toast, and fruit. I had missed her way of cooking and tried to enjoy the food while also trying to avoid Mr. Mark's astute gaze of concern swinging from Grandmother's face to my own.

"Jasmina, dear, would you get me a cup of tea?" Grandmother asked. "I've a dreadful headache, and I think some tea might be soothing."

On my way back from the kitchen, teacup in hand, I came close enough to hear Grandmother speaking in concerned tones. "I wish Dr. Andersen would return soon. When he left with the others to do the free clinic in the village, I was feeling much improved. But since then I seem to feel worse."

"Your hip still hurts you?"

I stopped before coming through the doorway, not sure why I waited for Grandmother to answer Asha's question.

"Not only my injured hip, but the other as well. And my joints all over my body. And I'm getting miserable headaches." She reached across and grasped Mr. Mark's hand. "And the nightmares. Horrible. Last night I dreamed Amrita was killed and Jasmina came bursting in here covered in blood. I'm starting to wonder if I'm going crazy."

Mr. Mark glanced up and saw me in the doorway. I took a step back.

"We'll call Dr. Andersen this morning and ask him if he can come back from the clinic before the others," he said.

"And we're going to stay with you too," Asha added. My heart did a strange jump in my chest. I had not even thought of the fact that with Asha and Mr. Mark back, I would be expected to return to their home with them. It was at least two hours' drive distant from the compound and the city. J would never be able to contact me there. Phone reception did not even work out there.

"No, dears, you need to go to your home. You've been gone so long."

I peeked to see Asha shake her head at Grandmother's objection. "We'll go home for a day to get some things and so Mark can do some of the work that is piling up. Then we'll come back here and stay with you until you are well."

She did not say what I knew she was thinking, what I was thinking as well. Someone had to stay with Grandmother in case her mind wandered again. She was in her own kind of danger and did not even know it.

The dishes were cleared and after enjoying her tea, Grandmother and Asha went for a morning walk with the baby. I found myself sitting at the table across from Mr. Mark in an uncomfortable silence. I looked at his kind smile and thought again how, if it was permissible to say about a man, how beautiful he was with his light skin and hair the color of sunshine in the morning. Even though I had heard him speak a hundred times, it still always surprised me a little when fluent Bangla came from his mouth.

"Jasmina, can you tell me about my Grandmother, please?" His voice was always so polite, never aggressive like American voices tended to be. "When we found out she had broken her hip, we changed our tickets for an earlier flight back, but I didn't expect to find her so . . ."

"I know." He did not need to speak the words.

"What kind of medicine did Dr. Andersen give her?"

I shared the information I had gleaned from watching and listening, a trait of nosiness necessary when one is too young to comfortably question an elder. "She was in much pain at first and having difficulty sleeping because of the pain. Dr. Andersen gave her two bottles of pills. One for the pain. One for sleeping, if she needed it. After the third night, she put the sleeping ones away because she said she did not want to get—I don't remember—it was an English word that meant she did not want to start to need them."

"Addicted."

"Yes." I looked back at the door, making sure she had not yet returned. I felt I was shaming myself by betraying a confidence, but I knew Mr. Mark would want all the information I could give him. She was his real grandmother after all. "I have tried to watch carefully, and she does not take the pain pills more often than the doctor said, and she only takes one instead of two. I think she must have developed the sickness of the old."

His eyebrows came together, and I feared he was angry, but then I remembered it was his way when thinking. "Thank you, Jasmina. And thank you for staying here. It must have been hard on you."

I put my eyes down in deference, not trusting myself to speak aloud that yes, it had been hard. I missed the steady presence of my friend, her wisdom about life, her love for God. Since her injury, we had not had our nightly Bible readings more than once or twice. I had read my Bible alone, calling out to God to bring her mind back. I was not ready to say goodbye to her yet.

But I had not been ready to say goodbye to Amrita either. Was I praying wrong somehow? Who could I ask about such a thing if not Grandmother?

"I'm sorry to ask this of you," Mr. Mark continued, his eyebrows even closer together than before, "but do you think you could manage here with Grandmother today and tomorrow? I need to go home and get my materials to translate, and we need to visit several people, but I can't leave her here alone."

"Of course I will stay," I put in quickly. He asked about my father and what J had said about which brick kiln he was in, and then promised to call the international liaison on their way out of the city to see if he could get started finding the kiln and planning a rescue. I thanked him and wanted to tell him about J promising to contact me about Mother, but I did not want to add to his burden. I could tell them about J's plan to find my mother when they returned.

"You have been a blessing to us, Jasmina." His kind smile was back, and I found myself fighting tears. "We thanked God for you many times during our weeks in America." His smile dropped. "I wish we could have spared you what happened last night."

"Don't fuss at her, Mark."

I jolted from my chair and turned to see Asha's hand on the open doorknob, baby Adiya balanced on her hip, and Grandmother already inside. Grandmother continued speaking, "I know you had your reservations about Jasmina working alongside Amrita, and quite frankly I still do. Amrita is sometimes fearless to the point of recklessness. None of us want Jasmina to be led into danger."

My hands gripped the chair until I wondered if it might break from the pressure. "Grandmother . . ."

"I want you to know I am proud of you, Jasmina." Grandmother approached me and put a hand on my shoulder. I fought to keep my face clear of emotion and my eyes dry. "You have shown a clear head in difficult situations, and that, along with your desire to help people in need, is a gifted combination that God will use for great things."

My throat closed up. When she hugged me to her, I allowed my face to show the agony I felt, emotions I saw mirrored on Asha's face as she watched. Baby Adiya gurgled and tried to eat her fist.

"I'm feeling quite worn out these days," the elderly woman said as she released me. "I'd like to take a nap, and then after these young people leave for their trip, would you join me Jasmina for some Bible reading? I know I've been sleeping more these days, and I've missed our nightly talks."

The tears did come then. I hoped she would see them as care for her for they were. "I have as well."

"Good, then I shall not feel so lonely saying goodbye to my loved ones so soon after their return. They will come back soon, and in the meantime you will still be with me."

"Yes, Grandmother." I gripped the chair again. "I will stay with you."

My Fateful Decision

Asha, Mr. Mark, and baby Adiya left that afternoon with Grandmother and me waving from the window of her home. We read together that night, I with hope in my heart. Mr. Mark had called us right before supper. He had talked with Grandmother, and then asked to talk with me.

With surprise, I had taken the phone from Grandmother's outstretched hand and put it up to my ear, ignoring the sudden flashback of holding Amrita's phone to that same ear, screaming into it for help. I had not yet told Grandmother about Amrita. She was having a lucid day and I could not upset her.

"Y-yes? Hello?" I spoke at the phone.

"Jasmina, I have important news." Mr. Mark usually went through the formalities of polite conversation, so it surprised me that he got directly to the point. All those weeks in America had probably brought back his Western habits. "It took all this time to finally get through to Dr. Andersen. He's coming back early from the clinic to see Grams. He should get in by dark tomorrow. But listen, we're almost to the point where the phone signal will die out, so I need to say this fast."

"Or you could just pull over," I heard Asha say in the background.

"Good idea. Just a second, Jasmina."

I waited without speaking, listening to the sounds coming through the phone as Mr. Mark likely had to nudge his way through people and animals to find a spot on the side of the road to park. I looked to where Grandmother had lowered herself to recline on the couch and gave her a confident smile I did not feel. He said he had news. About what? Grandmother's condition or mine? Had he heard anything from the sunglasses man about my father?

"Okay, are you there?"

I put the phone close to my ear again. "Yes."

"I said all of this to Grams, but I want to tell you in case she forgets." I winced, hoping he had not said such to her. "Dr. Andersen said her symptoms all sound like she got her bottles of pills mixed up. He thinks she's been taking the sleeping pills instead of the pain pills. They are not to be taken more than once a day, and even at that, if you take them every day for a while, they can cause all those problems."

"Then it might be just the medicine?"

"He thinks so. You need to make sure she doesn't take any of those pills any more. Can you do that?"

How was I to do that? It was unthinkable that I would go up and snatch them from her hands. She had the bottle in hand now, looking it over, holding it up to the light as if looking for clues to a mystery.

"Yes," I heard myself say. Of course I had to say it. I could not refuse him. "But how will I—"

"Good," he said, and I heard the background noise getting louder. "We've got a lot of vendors all around the car now. I'm going to need to get going before we're stuck here. Thank you again, Jasmina. Hopefully by the time we get back tomorrow, she'll be doing a lot better."

I closed the phone and handed it back to Grandmother, feeling a nauseating mixture of determination and self-disgust.

I had to get those pills. They were hurting her and possibly causing her life to be in danger. But how?

"My dear." Grandmother stood, pill bottle in hand. "I want you to take these pills and flush them down the toilet."

My jaw dropped, and she smiled. I took the bottle she held out to me, and she walked me across the room and toward the hall. "We'll do it together, shall we? Mark says I may have gotten the pills switched on accident." She shook her head. "It's no wonder. They should have had the sense to make them different colors at least for old ladies like me." She rubbed her fingers against her forehead. "And here I'd put the other ones away because I didn't want to get addicted to them. They might have actually helped my hip feel better!"

I laughed in sheer relief as we opened the bottle and dumped all its contents into her Western sit-down toilet and watched them swirl down and away when she pushed the lever. The poor girl in me hated the waste; were I still on the street I could have sold that medicine and used the money for food. However, the larger part of me, the part that loved this woman at my side, was glad to see them disappear.

"Oh, I had one or two pills laid out on my bedside table, too, for when I woke in the night. Get those for me, will you?"

We flushed those as well, and I hoped she had not stashed any more in other places. After she went to sleep that night, I searched the house for any others, afraid she might forget and take them out of habit.

I did not search well enough, as I would discover the following morning. I had awoken early after a fitful sleep full of dreams of Amrita and the man wearing sunglasses. Before doing anything else, I reached for my Bible, the Bangla one Mr. Mark had given me when I first came to stay with them, and asked God to give me something to help me cope with my sorrow and my guilt. I had not yet asked for something to help with my pain over my brother's willingness to abandon me to save himself or the horrific possibility that he, though not yet fifteen, was already a man willing to kill.

Grandmother had taught me to search the Psalms in moments of sorrow or confusion of heart. The king who wrote the Psalms knew great despair, and his words of how he wept through the night and how God kept his tears in a book soothed some of the ache that I wondered would ever go away. I had so much I needed to ask Asha about death, about Amrita. How was I to keep on living when she could not?

I could ask Grandmother. If she was thinking clearly again, she would understand. I needed to tell her about Amrita anyway, much as I dreaded sharing such news, but then I could ask what I should do with the fears that flew through me and seemed never to land in one place long enough for me to take them captive.

Wearing the same shalwar kameez as I had the day before, but at least with brushed hair this time, I left the bedroom and started for the kitchen, detouring when I saw the front door wide open. Had she gone outside?

"Grandmother?" I stepped out through the front door and looked left and right but saw no one except Dapika, who was walking from the orphanage building toward the playground behind it. She waved and I returned the gesture, my eyes already back on the area around me. I walked all the way around the house, even checking behind the large bush, but found nothing unusual.

My steps took me back to the front door, which was now closed. Confusion caused my hand to hesitate as I reached for the knob, and as I did, the door swung open. Grandmother stared at me, wide-eyed, her hair a riotous mess.

"Hurry!" she whispered. "Get inside!"

When I did not move, she reached out and dragged me in, slamming the door closed. She pushed me toward the kitchen. "I know just where to hide you. They'll be here soon. Hurry!"

Oh no. She was nudging me toward the kitchen sink, and I knew with sudden clarity that she was remembering the time she rescued a woman from a terrible suttee death by hiding her in the cupboards under her kitchen sink. She had told me the story several times over the past week. But that was when she lived in a place where the cupboards were bigger! She must have had another pill or two stashed somewhere and taken them. What was I going to do?

"Grandmother." My voice squeaked.

"Your grandmother isn't here, dear," Grandmother said, pushing me forward. "You have to trust me. God is going to protect you."

I looked up in silent plea to God, not really for protection, but for a little wisdom. We arrived at the kitchen sink, and Grandmother's face wrinkled in bewilderment. "Who put everything back in these cupboards?"

I looked down and breathed out a near-hysterical laugh. The cupboards, far too small for me to fit in, were full of cleaning supplies and a trash can.

"That man," Grandmother huffed. "Can't stand for anything to be left out for half an hour. Why I remember one time . . ." She began a story of her husband, who died years ago, and I thought I was safe from an impossibly tight squeeze into the cupboards, but then she stopped herself. "No, no," she said, "I mustn't get distracted. We have to get you into those cupboards before those villains arrive!"

Leaving the cupboards open, I turned, touched her elbow and led her toward the hallway. "Let's go hide in your room," I said. We could sit on her bed and maybe she would fall asleep. "I'd feel safer in there with you."

"Good idea," she agreed, grasping my hand and stepping ahead to pull me behind her. "We'll hide in the bathroom. It has a lock on the door. No one will think to look for us there."

Indeed, no one did think to look for us there. We huddled on the hard tile floor all morning, Grandmother telling stories of her husband to help me keep from panicking. I appreciated her effort, and I felt near panicking several times, though not for the reasons she assumed. I prayed silent prayers that God would help us. Grandmother interrupted one of my prayers to assure me, "Safety is of the Lord, dear child. Even walking through the valley of the shadow of death, we need fear no evil, for God is with us." Then her eyes lit up, and her smile turned mischievous. "And to get to you, those ruffians will have to face me first, and I pack a mean wallop."

Tears stung my eyes. I wished for Mr. Mark or, better yet, Dr. Andersen. "I'm not ready to lose you," I heard myself whisper. "I still have so many questions, so much I need to know."

"Speak up, dear," she said beside me.

I pulled my knees up to my chest and laid my head down in the ridge formed between them. "Would you tell me more about your husband?" I asked.

Summoned

I know not how many hours we sat on the bathroom floor, but when I heard Dapika's voice approaching the house and jumped up into a standing position, my legs barely held my weight. My hinder parts ached, and then pin pricks spread up from my feet to my knees in unpleasant protest.

"Dapika!" I yelled. "We're in here!"

Grandmother rose much slower than I had. "Oh, these old bones don't like such hard floors. Let's hide someplace softer next time."

With hearty agreement, I helped her steady herself. "Is it safe?" she asked. "Are they gone?"

"The bad guys are not here," I said, knowing it to be true. They were about a mile away, trafficking people for a living, on the lookout for me. "We can come out now."

"Oh, thank the Lord. I'm so hungry."

Her comment made me laugh, and I was surprised to hear the sound. The guilt that hovered around me flooded in again. Amrita was gone. I should not be able to laugh. I should not want to laugh.

We emerged from Grandmother's room just as the knock sounded on the door. "It's them again!" Grandmother cried out and clung to me.

"No, it's okay. It's only Dapika."

"Oh." Grandmother stood straight again and headed for the kitchen. "Is she a friend of yours? Do invite her to stay for lunch. You can help me cook, but beware these burners. They get mighty hot." She put her hands to her hips. "Now who left these cupboards open?"

I left her rummaging through the refrigerator and went to open the door. I nearly hugged Dapika with relief. "I need your help," I said, pulling her inside much as Grandmother had done to me earlier.

Dapika shook her head at me. "First, you need this." She handed me a piece of paper, folded many times to make a small square that fit in the palm of her hand. "It's a message for you."

I picked it up and turned it over. Never in my life had I received a personal message. My fingers clumsy with haste, I opened the folds and looked down to the last word on the paper. It was not a word, but one letter.

"J." He had said he would find some way to contact me. "How did you get this?"

"Some street kid brought it to the gate and said it was for you." Dapika shrugged. "Milo's dad gave it to Milo, and he gave it to me."

"Did you read it?"

Her chin went up. "Of course not." I began to apologize, but she stopped me with a grin. "Actually I wanted to, but Milo made me promise I wouldn't."

I skimmed over the note, and then read it slowly, thinking over each word. "He knows the address," I said in a breath. "He knows where my mother is." All these years, all my searching. It was almost over.

"Is he going to get her?"

My fingers shook with excitement as I handed the letter over to Dapika. "He says I'm to meet him tonight at a house outside the city, and then we'll go together to the house where my mother is kept as a slave."

Dapika frowned at the note. "He doesn't say what you will do when you get there, or how you'll get her out."

"That was likely to keep the information safe just in case the note was intercepted. He has a plan, I know. I trust him."

Dapika nodded. "Amrita sent him on this mission after all."

With a cringe I realized no one on the compound knew what had happened to Amrita. I had not told them, so how would they know? Asha and Mr. Mark left before really talking with many people there, and all the missionaries were away at the clinic.

"My dears." Grandmother appeared nearby. "Would one of you go call my husband and tell him lunch is ready?"

"Oh no," I said when she retreated to the kitchen again. "Dr. Andersen won't be here until tonight. What am I going to do? J says I'm to meet him right at sunset."

"Did she just ask us to go get her husband?" Dapika was staring at the entrance to the kitchen.

"I'll explain later."

We helped prepare a very odd lunch concocted from every leftover in Grandmother's refrigerator, all topped with a strange sauce Mr. Mark had brought her back from America called mustard. As we ate, she told us of all the different kinds of mustard at the stores in America, interspersed with stories of her husband, her son, and grandson, and one random Bible verse after she ate her last bite. Dapika kept casting questioning looks my way, but I continued to beam my fake smile toward Grandmother until we had cleaned up the table and she excused herself for a nap. I had no time to check her room for any more pills, but I did follow and keep watch as she settled into bed without drinking anything. She would likely wake up her normal self with no recollection of the morning.

Dapika was sitting on the couch when I returned to the main room, my hand to my aching head. "What is going on with her?" she asked. "Was that all some sort of game?"

"I wish it was only that," I said with a sigh, telling Dapika everything. Had I been given a choice, I would have kept Grandmother's secret until Dr. Andersen could arrive and set things right. But now with J's note and the urgent need to leave, I had to confide in Dapika and ask her to stay with Grandmother through the afternoon and evening until Dr. Andersen came. Grandmother could not be left alone. I feared for her safety, especially if she planned to cook supper on her old stove, or if the power went out and she needed to light some candles.

"Would you stay here with her? I'll have to leave soon to make sure I am there in time. It is some distance."

"Shouldn't you talk with Asha about this first? Or Amrita?"

I swallowed. "You said yourself Amrita is the one who sent J to find out where my parents were. And Asha is at home out of cell phone range. I still don't know how to send those messages from Grandmother's computer to theirs, so what can I do?"

Dapika tugged on her braided hair. "What about the international man with the sunglasses?"

"I can't call him. I don't know his number." I moved to sit on the couch and Dapika shifted to give me room. "Please, Dapika. I'd ask if there was anyone to ask, but the only adults on the compound are Milo's father and the guy who cuts the grass. And Grandmother, but you can see why I can't ask her."

"And you say Dr. Andersen will be here by tonight?"

I stood. "Yes, and Mr. Mark and Asha are coming back tomorrow."

She stood as well. "And when would you be back?"

"I don't know. Hopefully tonight." With my mother. Both hope and fear bubbled to the surface. "Since it's far, maybe not until tomorrow."

"You can't stay overnight somewhere, not without a chaperone!"

An exasperated breath escaped. "And who is going to chaperone me? Milo?" I bit my lip and felt the scab developing there. “I have to go, and I have to go today. There’s no time to call someone to come and no one nearby to ask. I lived on the streets before. I can handle one night in some rich neighborhood outside the city.”

Dapika tugged on her hair again. “I don’t like it,” she said.

Her words, the exact ones I had said standing with Amrita before she got shot, gave me pause. Should I not go? Should I wait until I could talk with Asha?

I shook my head and put a hand on Dapika’s arm. “It’s my mother, Dapika. I haven’t seen her for so many years, and I may never have this chance again. Would you wait?”

For the first time I saw tears form in her eyes. “No,” she said. “I wouldn’t.”

“Then you’ll stay with Grandmother for me?”

She nodded. “Let me go explain to Milo and ask him to take charge of the kids the rest of the day.” At my look, she added, “I’ll only tell him she’s sick and needs someone to look after her until the doctor comes.”

With little patience I waited for Dapika’s return, my thoughts filled with images and memories and questions. I would rescue my mother tonight, and Mr. Sunglasses might be working on a plan to rescue my father soon as well. Was my father sorry for what he did to us all? Would I even know it if he was? He said little when we were children, and most of what he did say was directed at Samir, his heir. What would Samir think when he found out they had been rescued? He wanted them to suffer for all they had made us suffer, and a certain part of me longed for that as well, but I knew it was wrong. I would pray. All the way there, I would pray for my father and my mother, and for myself for courage the moment we finally stood face-to-face again after all these years.

We would stand face-to-face . . . and then what would happen?

twenty-four
The Neighborhood

Dapika took so long that by the time she returned, I was pacing. Her entrance was met by a quick set of instructions from me for Grandmother's care before I went running toward the gate. I had changed into a dark outfit, in case I needed to avoid being seen at some point, and packed a bag with one bottle of water from Grandmother's refrigerator, two mangoes, and the money J had enclosed in his note for the expense of traveling to the address given.

The last time I had taken food from Grandmother's house, I did so as a thief, a desperate one. This time my conscience was not disturbed, for Grandmother said I was welcome to anything in her kitchen. I was to see her home as my own, and as the weeks had passed, I had indeed begun to see it that way. When I found my parents and they were freed, would all of that change?

I had told myself I would pray on the ride to the address, and pray I did, not leaving room for thoughts of my unknown future and how tenuous my own freedom to think and make choices might become by the end of this night.

I took an auto, choosing a longer, bumpier ride over a bus crowded with people, any of whom might recognize my face. I braced myself for the auto's quick swerves around rickshaws and pedestrians carrying live chickens or hats for sale, feeling much like I used to in those rare moments my father took me out on his boat and the waves lifted and dropped the tiny craft like a toy, only in the auto the tossing was side to side. My hands gripped the edging around the open doorway, but still I banged my head several times before we finally left the chaos of the city. I looked in wonder over miles of rice fields, more grass and field than I had ever seen of a green color so vibrant no painter could reproduce it. Tiny huts, like the one I grew up in, dotted the landscape far from the road, looking like small playthings a child had made from sticks. A few people could be seen gathering rice inside small, square plots of land, their feet immersed in water up to their calves, the thin green shoots reaching up through the water to poke their ends out as if trying to catch a breath.

We rode on, and the green faded, burned into a deeper hue by the setting sun. I stuck my head out through the doorway and looked up. I had been so transfixed by the sights of the world outside the city I had not noticed how late it had become. Were we almost there?

The auto turned off the main road, and we bounced over gravel and dirt—not what I would have expected to lead to a neighborhood where people were rich enough to own slaves. Perhaps J wanted to meet in a safer place first and travel to the neighborhood together. Fear, slippery eel that it is, began to slither down my spine until I shivered. I prayed. Uncertain what to pray for, I simply asked God for help. I asked for courage. And I dared to ask for love. That my parents would love me and be glad to see me, or at least be grateful for all I sacrificed to rescue them. Father would surely blame me for Samir's absence. I was the elder and expected to take care of him. But that could not be helped at this point. I would explain, leaving out as much as possible about Samir's wrong choices. It would make me look worse in Father's eyes, but it would spare him the shame of knowing his son had chosen a life of evil. I could sacrifice my own value in his eyes for that. I must.

Something in me prayed my mother would see past my words and understand that things were not as they seemed. I had considered bringing my diary with me, the notebook I had written for her when I thought I might die having the kidney operation. If we had little to say on the drive back, she could read it, I reasoned, and know my heart and many of the words I could not say. But it would be dark by then, and I did not want to risk losing it, so I had left it behind.

The auto stopped, and I corralled my thoughts to the present place and time. I stepped from the little vehicle, looked around, and gasped. It looked darker from where I stood, but not because the sun had set; the light was hidden behind towering mansions standing in a line before me. We had come to the back of the neighborhood on a road for servants or peddlers—those who did not expect and should not think they deserved a smoothly paved road like the one on the front side.

I looked all around, mystified. Behind me as far as I could see lay rice fields and nothing else save a few palm trees. I could not see past the line of houses. Was there a town nearby? Or had these wealthy people chosen to live far away from the city, avoiding the pollution and noise and millions of bodies and souls crammed into small spaces?

Who were the people who lived here in homes three or four stories high? It could not be people like Gar, wealthy but only so long as he continued his trade. Were these the kind who bought and sold positions like Gar's, controlling the trafficking industry without having to directly soil their hands?

Or perhaps they were just rich people who did not know where slaves came from and did not think their servants capable of wanting more than scraps and scoldings. I knew from experience on the streets that people treated other people based on how they viewed them. If they saw another person as an animal, they treated the person as an animal. People had often looked at me either with pity or with greed, and I learned quickly to recognize each kind, to utilize the pity and flee the greed. Not until I met Asha and Grandmother and the others did I learn that one can be looked at and treated with love, even by a stranger, for those who love with God's love do not need to know a person's status before deciding her value.

I needed to remember that this night. If I had to face people whose homes were worth more money than I would see my entire life, I had to remember I was not worth less because I had less or because my skin would surely be dark as dirt compared to their high-class avoid-the-sun coloring or that my parents were only lowly slaves. I would stand tall, knowing I had a value greater than any superficial sign of status could give. I was adopted by God into His family, which meant I was a daughter of the King of earth and heaven. I would not cower before money or status or even evil.

Unwittingly, I had clenched the paper so tightly in my hand, it remained a clumped ball when I opened my fist. I spread it out and read the address one more time, paid the driver with J's money, and then took a deep, deep breath. Tonight I would help set my parents free, and my search would be over, freeing me as well.

Such was my hope. Such was my fear.

I walked forward.

twenty-five
The Unfinished House

Had I read the address right? I kept to a path behind the houses, not wanting to draw attention. A look through the spaces between houses as I darted from one landscaped backyard to the next sometimes showed me a house number on a large fake rock or a special sign near the road's edge. I followed the trail of numbers leading to the house at the far end of the street, set apart somewhat from the others on the downward slope of a small hill.

Mr. Mark had taught me an English phrase that I used at that moment. "This place gives me the creeps," I said, looking over the house down the hill from my position behind another, safer-looking structure. From my stance inside a shadow, the walls looked either abandoned or unfinished. The house appeared the same color as the bare earth around it, like a mountain of stone and glass rising from the ground, bronzed by the light of the setting sun.

I considered my options. From where I stood to the edge of the property bordering the last house, a line of trees would give me cover. Shoes in hand, for I had removed them before crossing one landscaped brick path, I crept bare-footed across the tickling grass to the trees aligned too perfectly to have been positioned there by nature. Slipping from behind one tree to another, I made my way across the yard without making or hearing any sound. I could see I would have to sprint across the remaining distance and just hope I was not seen. No one was outside. In fact, the neighborhood seemed empty of people. Perhaps the wealthy did not like the untreated outside air with its heat and humidity.

Two steps into my sprint, I heard a noise and quickly flattened myself on the ground. Turning to my left where the sound had come from, I saw a door open three houses down and a man emerge. He looked side to side, but did not see me lying on the ground in the shadow of the last tree. He closed the front door softly, as if trying to keep from disturbing anyone inside, then leaned back against the large front door and looked up toward the sky.

I waited for him to go inside. Was he a slave like my parents? If he could get out, why did he not escape? Maybe he was indentured and there by choice.

Long minutes passed. I had laid stomach down, and the grass prickled the skin of my neck and cheek, making it itch. A bug landed on my temple, and I scrunched my facial muscles trying to get it to fly off. It crawled along my skin, and, when I could bear it no longer, I reached up my hand and swiped it away, and then looked at the man. He did not turn or move, just continued looking up into the sky, as if wishing for an airplane to arrive and carry him away.

A sound to my right caught my attention. As quietly as I could, I turned my head to look toward the abandoned house, where I should have already been. A shadow moved. I saw a figure come toward the house from the opposite direction. My heart sped when I recognized J.

Please go inside, I begged silently, wishing my thoughts toward both J and the man standing outside the other house. If

J did not go inside, he might be seen. If the other man did not go inside, I surely would be.

Finally an impatient call came from inside the third house, and the man sighed and then carefully turned the doorknob and disappeared. The mansion, like a great whale, swallowed him whole.

I wasted no time. The moment the man was inside, I leaped to my feet and hurled my body toward the abandoned house. I ran around the back, stopping only once to put my sandals back on my feet, looking for any entrance other than the front door. A window low to the earth near the far side had been broken. The house must have been left unfinished, for the set of steel bars that should have lined the window lay below it in a pile on the ground. Careful to avoid the shards of glass edging the right side of the window, I put my left leg through the window then angled my body inside the narrow space, my right leg following once I had steadied myself.

Safely inside, I stood still for several minutes, listening for noises, any hint that someone had heard me and would come to investigate. Only the zinging sound of crickets and a few caws from crows met my ears. As I waited for my heart to return to its normal pace, I looked around. The setting sun was low, nearly horizontal now, shooting lines of light through the windows and across what would be a marvel of a home had it been completed. The tile beneath my feet had been laid in a mosaic pattern of circles and swirls, dark blues swirling around light blue, like waves or wind on the ocean. A hallway to my right hinted of several bedrooms, and to my left stood a massive marble staircase edged with black poles curving upward to a second floor. Past the staircase I saw two more large areas for rooms and a doorway that likely led to even more. An entire village could live in a house such as this, I mused, my hand finding the arm rail as I started up the stairs. Dust quickly filled my palm, and I lifted my hand, avoiding the rail the rest of the way up.

Where was J? I did not dare call out his name. On the second floor, I explored without fear, certain J and I were the only ones in this concrete block of wealth and beauty. A balcony off one of the rooms tempted me to wander out and view the glorious sunset draping the neighborhood in gold, but I refrained. I wanted to get to my mother as soon as possible, which meant I had to find J right away.

A smaller staircase along the left wall of the second floor's main area caught my attention. Had I arrived first, that is where I would have gone, so I followed the message of my instincts and climbed the stairs to the third floor.

"J?" I whispered as I reached the top of the stairs and looked around at a kind of attic. I had seen a room like this once in a movie at Asha's house. She told me some American homes have attics where people store the things they do not use. I never dreamed anyone in my country was rich enough to have so much more than they needed that they had to create an extra room for it all.

Along the facing wall, I saw one small window. An elongated box of light stretched from the window across the floor where much dust and a few old tools lay scattered. My gaze followed the light and across the room beyond it. No furniture, just a few wooden planks stacked outside the line of light.

"Jasmina."

I jumped and grabbed the railing to keep from falling down the stairs. "J?"

A figure far in the corner moved, and, despite the slight chill that ran through me, I smiled and stepped forward to meet him.

"I've been waiting for you," he said. My smile remained as he approached, right up until the moment he walked into the light and I saw the knife in his hand.

twenty-six
A Friendship Lost

"That's a big knife." I was proud that I kept my voice level. My hand involuntarily reached to my throat. "Is that the knife you had when . . . the night that . . ."

"It is." J was not smiling in welcome. His face held none of the pleased excitement I had expected.

"Will you need that when we go get my mother?" I asked, my eyes not able to leave the gleaming silver blade.

"I hope not."

I swallowed the fear rising in my throat and took a step toward him. "I'm ready. What is the plan to get my mother out? Will we be able to get her tonight? Where is she?"

He scowled and walked to look out the one small window. "She is kept in the house next to this one."

My veins surged with a feeling I could not name. My mother, so close, inside the house I had just hid behind on my way here. "Will we go—"

"Shh." J put a hand toward me but kept his eyes on the window. I clamped my mouth shut, and my eyes shifted back and forth, a useless effort to see whatever unnamed danger was making noise outside the mansion.

"Do you hear that?"

I listened. Yes. A crack, and then another, as if someone were walking outside the house and not taking care to avoid stepping on fallen sticks. My heart, which had finally stopped pounding from my rush there and climb to the third floor, picked up speed again. I joined J at the window and tried to see into the yard. A clang, sharp and loud, rose up from below and I pictured the steel bars lying outside the broken window, bars that would make that sound if someone had dropped one on the others, or if a bar had slid and fallen when someone stepped on them to get inside.

My shaking hands gripped J's arm. I was beyond the point of caring if he knew I was scared.

But my fear lifted from the danger below and shifted to the danger nearby when J removed my hands, turned me around, and, just as he had the night of Amrita's death, held his knife to my throat.

"Who is down there?" he whispered in my ear. I had heard the threat in his voice before, but never directed at me.

"J?" My hands had not found a place to settle. They shook in front of me, waving about, as if reaching for help from an invisible rescuer. His grip on me tightened, and though he did not move the knife closer to my skin, I clutched at his arm with my hands and pulled.

Another clang had me fearing both what was behind me and below me. "Be still," J ordered, and I obeyed. "Who is it?" he whispered again.

I shook my head. "I don't know." I heard the desperation in my voice. "I came alone." Why would J suspect otherwise? Who would I bring if not someone to help?

We waited beside the light of the window, my own heavy breathing matching his, silent and listening for signs that someone was inside the house with us.

"Is it your brother?" J whispered.

"Samir?" What would he have to do with this? I almost shook my head again but decided to stay still. J's grip was no longer tight, and the knife was not close, but I did not want to take any chances. "I don't understand. You said he didn't know the address."

"He does now. Gar told me this morning, and I know he told Samir too. He's got some plan, twisting all of us against each other. I'm not even sure your mother is next door. It may all be a trap."

My insides shook. "To trap me?"

I saw that the knuckles of his hand around his knife had gone white from gripping it so tightly. "Or to use you as bait to trap another."

Who was left to trap? "J, what is going on? I don't understand any of this. And would you please let me go and put the knife down? You're scaring me."

He released me with a sigh. Several minutes had passed without any sounds, and my body felt weak with relief. I turned to face him, and he spoke, looking at me hard as if gauging my response. "When Gar gave me the address for your mother, he told me if I handed you over to him, I would get the position Fayeed left behind when you got him arrested. I know he is testing me and Samir, so he probably gave the same information to him. Did you get a note from Samir today too?"

The parts inside me that had been shaking now twisted and knotted tight. "No, but I left soon after I got your note." I looked out the window but saw nothing. "You think Samir might be coming to find me here?" My gaze found his face again, and I could not read the thoughts behind his dark eyes. "Then we'd better help my mother quickly and get out. I don't want Samir to find us. He'd contact Gar and let him know we're here."

"I already contacted Gar." The words came through my ears and my mind understood all the sounds, but could not grasp that they all connected to mean the unthinkable.

"You—you did? But why?"

"He's coming in the morning." J's face was still unreadable, and I felt as if something within me cracked and began to bleed. "Samir will come sometime before then, wanting to hand you over and get the position himself."

"I don't—I don't—"

"We won't be getting your mother tonight, Jasmina. We will wait here until the morning. Until Gar comes."

twenty-seven
Shattered Trust

While I stood mute, crumbling on the inside, J took one final look out the window and then went to sit on the stack of boards. He considered the knife in his hand, and I considered his face. The face of a friend. The face of an enemy. If I could not trust him, I could trust no one. Now I understood how Amrita said she could never be free. Evil did not fight this battle fairly. It crushed and destroyed, and I was now a casualty.

"Come sit beside me, Jasmina." J's voice had lost its edge of warning, but when I remained still, closer to the stairs than to him, my gaze on the steps leading down to the second floor, he spoke more harshly. "I don't want to have to tie you up to make sure you don't run, but I will if I have to. Show me I don't have to by coming over here and sitting down."

Despite how broken my heart felt, I still feared my brother more than J, leaving me with little desire to run downward if downward meant possibly meeting up with Samir. I stepped over a broken board and made my way toward him. As I walked, my fear morphed into anger. How dare he do this to me? How dare he pretend to be my friend and gain my trust and then trap me here so close to what I had spent years trying to find?

My feet stopped. I could run. It was nearly dark and Samir, even if he was in the neighborhood, did not know where I was. If it had been him snooping below, he must have decided we were not here and moved on. I could run to the nearest house and plead for help. No, they would likely shoo me away as a street kid or beggar. I could hide until my mother left the house, and then we could escape together. No, she was probably never let out.

What about the house where the man had slipped outside? I could hide and wait for him and ask him to help me. What price I would have paid at that moment for a cell phone. I still did not know the number for the man with the sunglasses, but I could call Asha's number and leave a message that she would receive tomorrow on their way back to the city. I could call Grandmother, and if Dapika answered, I could enlist her help to contact someone, anyone, to come to my aid.

Oh, why had I rushed here without letting any adult know? I thought I was past foolishly running into danger on my own. But I had trusted J.

He had been watching me, seeing the anger rise like water heating to a steady boil. "Don't try to run," he said softly, guessing at my thoughts. "If you escaped tonight, Gar would be made a fool of by you again. Who do you think he would punish? Don't you think there's a reason he wanted to trap you right here where your mother is?"

All my ideas dissolved, and I stared at J, wide-eyed. Gar was indeed the snake at the top, and I had ignorantly thought I could outwit him and win. I had failed. There was a chance when Amrita was with me and when I thought J was my ally. Now, I had no recourse left.

"I trusted you," I whispered. "You're worse than Samir and Gar." I'd planned to say those words with biting sharpness, but they came out a little-girl whine. "At least they never pretended to care about me."

The muscles in his jaw twitched, and I saw the pulse in his neck beating hard. "Sit," he ordered, and I did. "Talk, Jasmina," he said, his words quiet but his tone steel. "If you value your life or your parents' lives, you will tell me everything."

Everything, he said. How much of everything? "From when you came into my life with all your lies?" I asked, acid in my voice. My stomach churned. I could not look at him anymore. What did he want to hear? My naiveté in trusting him this whole time? Did he want to gloat over how he had so successfully brought me into his net?

"Go back as far as you want." His mouth tipped. "We have hours to fill. Entertain me."

I fought the urge to cry. "Why don't you just take me to Gar and get it over with?"

"Can't."

"Why not?"

He almost smiled. "It's a secret, Jasmina. You'll have to wait. You might as well talk."

Throat sore from swallowing the tears that threatened to shame me—I would not give him the satisfaction of seeing me cry—I said, "I'll talk, but know that not one word is to entertain you."

I thought of Dapika telling stories to the orphans on the compound and of Milo interrupting to add flair and laughter to them. I thought of Grandmother reading me God's stories from the Holy Book, of how her voice brought to life a God who loved people and intervened on their behalf. I thought of Asha telling my story to baby Adiya, how I escaped the garment factory and found her, and how Adiya had clapped and squealed in delight at the drama in her voice though she understood not one word. Such joyful stories and happy memories, so far removed from what I was now required to do.

How many hours had to pass before morning came? Twelve? More? I would tell him my story, starting from the night I met him outside the orphanage building, from back when I looked at him as a friend. In the telling I would remember those I loved and those I had trusted. Perhaps J would feel the guilt he should as he listened. Perhaps he would learn all that was at stake, how important the fight against trafficking was, and how his giving in to its power could only destroy him.

My heart prayed as I began. I did not ask for the impossible. In truth I did not know what to ask for, once again finding myself far from my expectations and not knowing what to do. I asked for help, for mercy from the God who sets the captives free. Only this time, the mercy I asked for was not only for me, but for the parents I had wanted so badly to rescue, the mother who was now nearby and yet still so fully enslaved, and, if Gar succeeded in the morning, always would be.

twenty-eight
The Question

I sat exhausted and empty of words, my story finished, wondering how many hours I had talked into the night. J had sat silent through the telling, never once looking my way, his eyes always out the window toward the moonlight or on the knife in his hands.

I waited for him to speak but was surprised at his words when he did. "I believe you," he said, his gaze still forward. "But he said I would and not to trust myself."

"Who said?" I was surprised I could produce any more words with my mouth so dry my tongue felt thick. I cocked my head and tried to get a better view of J's face.

For the first time in hours, he turned toward me. His knife dropped to clatter on the floor near his feet. "Jasmina, I'm going to ask you this once, and I want you to tell me the truth even if it's the last thing in the world I want to hear."

I frowned. His strong hands grasped my shoulders, and he looked at me deeply. "Whose side are you on?"

I felt my head shake a little as my mouth tipped lower. "Wh-what?"

His eyes were intense, as if he was trying to discover a truth deep within me. "Did Gar somehow get to you and convince you to betray Amrita, perhaps in exchange for your parents' freedom or your brother's? Or was Gar going to capture and sell you, and this was your only way out? To spy and share information so Amrita and the international liaison would finally be caught?"

I sucked in a quick gasp but still felt as if all the air had left my lungs. "What are you saying?" Had he not heard any of the thousands of words I had just told him?

He was still looking at me with hard, dark eyes. "It's a pretty strong coincidence that you were with Amrita when she visited the madam, when she was discovered to be an enemy of the traffickers, and especially when she was shot."

My mouth let out some sound, like the moan of a small, helpless animal in a trap. "How can you say that?" He thought I was the one who betrayed Amrita?

J's mouth dipped on one side. "He also said you would cry, and I had to keep from letting that affect me."

My shaking hand lifted to my face to discover my cheeks were wet. I had started crying and not even realized it. "J . . ." I had told myself I would not cry in front of him.

"There's no use trying to convince me you're with us," J said. He shook his head and turned away from me, looking out the window again, looking at nothing. "If you are working with them, I just wanted to give you the chance to say so to my face."

Us. Them. Who was who?

"But I thought . . . but then why would you . . ." I was so confused I could not find words. Was he asking if I was on Gar and Samir's side? Why on earth would I be?

I will never know why I did not force my mind to develop the questions into spoken words or why I did not try to escape while J's knife remained ignored on the floor. Instead, baffled and weary, with J's pained eyes still turned away from me, I methodically cleared a small area on the floor nearby, moving rusty tools and wood shavings and chips of dried paint until there was room for me to curl up into a ball like I used to on the street at night. I lay down, pulling my orna from my shoulders to use as a thin, meager blanket. With the edge of the material, I covered my face and hid, from J and his accusations, from my confusion over who was enemy and who was friend, and from my need to know why I was there and what would happen come morning. I prayed again, silently, and a strange and impossible peace came, cloaking me so much better than my flimsy orna could.

In the darkness touched lightly by the moon, in J's silence and my own uncertainty, I slept.

At first when I awoke, I wondered if Grandmother would recognize me or if she had found more pills hidden somewhere. When my eyes opened and no light reached them, I realized it must still be night and rolled over to find a more comfortable position to go back to sleep.

A more comfortable position was not to be had. My head banged against a hard surface, and my legs encountered an ankle that was not mine.

Considering the fact that I was accustomed to sleeping in a room alone, another person's presence was cause for alarm. As I flailed and sat up, my mind grasped upon the reality around me. It was still dark and I was still trapped in a mansion with J, who was waiting to deliver me over to my worst enemy.

"Oh," I moaned, rubbing my head where it had hit a wooden plank. "It wasn't a dream." I looked over to where J sat in exactly the same position he was in when I fell asleep. "Have you been up all night?" I asked, annoyed with myself that I would even care enough to ask. "What time is it?"

He smiled down on me. I wanted to kick him, or cry again.

"Good morning, Jasmina," he said cordially, as if he was not a betrayer. "Are you hungry?"

My stomach chose that moment to gurgle, and he laughed. I scowled at him. "Yes, I'm hungry. Did you bring breakfast?"

"No." He shrugged. "But you did." He pointed to my bag, long forgotten by me, dropped when J had grabbed me there at the window the night before. "I thought I saw a couple of mangoes in there," he added.

"You mean you snooped and found them." I could feel my face wrinkling like a prune at him. "May I go get them, or would you like to tie me up so you can get them?"

He grinned. "I won't tie you up, Jasmina. In fact, after doing some thinking, I've decided things might not be as bad as they seem."

I snatched up my bag and brought it back to where he sat. I gave up a silent prayer of thanksgiving for the bottle of water I pulled out. Twisting the cap off, I took a long drink and sighed. Then I handed the bottle to J. As much as I did not want to be nice to him, I remembered Grandmother reading Jesus' words to His followers, how we were to do good to our enemies. Were it Gar, I do not know if I could have offered a drink to him, but, according to J, he would be coming that morning, so I might still have the unfortunate opportunity to find out.

"Thanks." J took the bottle and enjoyed a drink. Then he reached into the bag for the two mangoes. "Good thing I brought my knife, huh?"

I thought of saying something sarcastic but decided not to waste the effort. Fatigue competed with the soreness in my muscles for the most unpleasant aspect of the morning. I wondered how long it would be before the sun came up, how much longer we would wait, and why I felt impatient, considering what we waited for was awful.

J cut into the mangoes, and we ate in silence. I used my orna to wipe the juice from my hands, not wanting to waste one drop of our precious bottle of water to wash them. Had the house been a little closer to finished, I might have searched for a fancy bathroom with running water.

The thought of a bathroom reminded me I was in need of one. I said such to J, and his friendly demeanor vanished. He gathered up our mango peels and gave them to me, and then he picked up his knife and led the way downstairs, me behind him with my palms full of dripping mango peels. I suppose he was keeping my hands outstretched and contained, using mangoes rather than handcuffs. We discovered a bathroom on the second floor, half-finished, with toilets and the beginnings of a sink but only stacks of tile where the bathing area should be. It was a pleasant surprise to find that the water worked, at least in a trickle. After I used the Indian floorboard toilet and flushed the mango peels down the Western-style one—why would anyone need both kinds in one bathroom?—I exited the room empty-handed, and J immediately grasped my wrist in one of his strong hands. "Wait here," he commanded. He looked me over with a frown. "How do I know you're not going to run away while I'm in there?"

I would have enjoyed his dilemma had I not been thinking of doing just what he said. He looked around the area outside the bathroom until his gaze fixed on a corner piled high with dusty ceramic tiles. "Come on." He dragged me there, pointed out a position, and waited while I tripped over tiles to stand in the middle of the pile. Doing so made an unpleasant racket, letting us both know his idea was smart. I would not be able to make my way out of the pile without making enough noise to warn him.

Arms crossed and scowl in place, I stood in my corner until J opened the bathroom door, hair wet and looking much refreshed. I should have thought to wash my face and get the dust out of my hair and off my arms too, though it would have been wasted effort I realized, as I climbed out of the pile of tiles and kicked up enough dust to coat me once more. I coughed. "I need a drink of water."

"Then we'll head back upstairs now." J resumed his grip on my wrist, and we climbed the stairs. I could not help but compare his current touch with how he had held my hand the night Amrita was shot. The lack of sleep and certain danger had my emotions simmering close to the surface. I begged my body not to shame itself by crying in front of him again.

We got to the top, and J looked down at his hand clamped around my wrist, as if he had been remembering too. "You know, it's easy to break out of a hold like this," he said, surprising me by setting down his knife, which I noticed he must have washed clean in the bathroom. "See where my thumb reaches around to connect with my other fingers?"

I nodded mutely.

"That's always a weak area." He took my other hand and positioned my fingers around his wrist to demonstrate. "If I pull against the force of your whole hand, trying to break free, I can only pull away if I am stronger than you. However, if I pull through that weak area . . ." He then jerked his hand against where my thumb met my fingers and easily released my hold. "No matter how much smaller you are, your arm is stronger than that weak point. See?"

He wrapped his hand around my wrist again, and I gave it a try, enjoying the small surge of power I felt when my hand yanked from his. "Try it again," he said, for some reason smiling at my success.

"Why are you doing this?" I asked. It made no sense that he, my captor, would want to teach me ways to get free.

He looked down at our arms, connected by his grasp on my wrist again. "If you do end up back on the wrong side, with the traffickers," he said, his voice sorrowful, "you will be in danger. If you ever wanted to get out, I would like to know I had helped you get away."

Oh, those stupid tears. "J—"

"So let me teach you something else." His voice was back to brusque and neutral. "Here, see this place on the side of my knee?" He patted his leg. "It's a vulnerable spot. If someone grabs you, hitting or kicking at them in general will not do you any good. But if you can land a solid kick to the side of my knee here, you immobilize me enough to get a running start." He demonstrated with a gentle push of his foot against mine, and I felt my leg easily give way.

He showed me if someone were to grab my hair, how to twirl underneath their grip and attack. "Self-defense is all about you becoming fiercer than whoever has you. The moment you are attacked, if you become a force ready to fight, you have a chance. Make noise, use anything around you for a weapon, look the person in the eye and shout at them. Do anything to show you are not going to cower and let them control you."

I thought of how the night had passed with me under his control. "What if a guy has a knife to your throat?" I asked, once again hoping for anger in my tone and hearing only hurt.

He looked down at his feet. "That's different," he said. "If there's a knife or gun involved, don't get yourself killed." Then he looked out the window. "But if you can cause a distraction and wriggle free, kick the guy's knee like I showed you and run. Even if there is a gun, it's hard to shoot a moving target, so run and keep running, shouting the whole time, until you get someplace safe."

"Why pretend you care if I'm safe?" I crossed my arms again, not wanting to play this game any longer. "The moment you hand me over to Gar, I'll never be safe again."

He ran a hand through his hair, releasing tiny droplets of water that caught the early morning light and sparkled as they fell. "Jasmina, I'm not . . ." He sighed and shook his head. "In just a few hours, you and I will both know what is really going on. For now, let's see if you learned what I taught you."

With a swift movement, he shifted behind me and had my hair in his hand, pulling back. My first reaction was to go with the force of his motion, letting him control me exactly as he had said. Instead, I clenched my teeth together, balled my fists, and swung my body around to face him, landing a hard punch right into his stomach. He had not taught me that, and it felt good to see him double over, surprise across his face. I started to run past him, and he reached out a hand and grabbed my wrist, a grip I easily wrenched free of by utilizing his weak point. I lifted my leg and aimed for the side of his knee.

"No, don't." J was upright again and held out both hands. "I don't want a broken leg." He smiled at me. "You're a fast learner."

I was not. I stood there, knowing at that moment I could kick him and run. His knife was across the room on the floor. I could get out of the house before he could catch me. So why was I still standing there, enjoying his approval? Just as he said, I was letting him control me. I was a coward, prisoner to my need to know who he was really working for, if there was some chance he was still the good friend I believed him to be.

"J, what is really going on?" I asked, my throat tight. "Who—"

We both froze at the sound coming from below. The sound of feet on broken glass and then the *pad, pad, pad* of footsteps on stairs.

J looked at me. "Someone is here."

The Fight

"Jasmina?"

I heard the whisper and started shaking. There was no question it was Samir's voice. J's eyes on mine, half-closed with scrutiny, made it clear he did not trust me. He turned me and positioned me at the top of the stairs. "Stand there," he whispered. "Respond to him and answer his questions, but do not move from this spot." He crossed the room and picked up his knife, holding it out and ready.

My trembling fingers gathered a handful of material at the front of my shalwar kameez and wadded it into a ball. "Sa-Samir, I'm here," I said, not sure my squeak was loud enough for him to hear. "I'm here," I repeated with more force, though alerting him to my presence was the last thing I wanted to do.

"Jasmina? Where?" I heard him reach the top of the stairs to the second floor.

"The third floor."

Though I knew it was him, when he appeared at the bottom of the stairs, I fought terror. Now I had two people holding outstretched knives looking at me. At least Gar was not with him yet. His heavy footsteps would have been easy to recognize.

"Did you get my message?" Samir asked.

He began to climb the stairs, and I put a hand out. "Stay there," I said. "Please."

"I gave it to someone at Amrita's salon," he continued, remaining where he was on the fourth step. "I didn't know where you lived, but they said they would get it to you."

"What do you want?" I asked, trying to keep my voice from shaking the way my insides were.

"Like I said in the message, I have a plan." He looked down at his knife. "I want out, Jasmina. I know you probably don't believe me. I know I've done terrible things and don't deserve another chance. But Gar has gone too far too many times. I don't want to be part of it anymore."

My mouth dropped open when he tucked his knife into his belt. He took another two steps up toward me, and I involuntarily took two steps back. "I've wanted out ever since the organ traffickers almost killed that girl." He shrugged and for a moment looked like the little boy I used to collect seashells with on the beach. "I may have been willing to steal and cheat, but I'm no killer." He put both hands in the pockets of his pants and looked up at me. "But Gar won't let me go. If I try to get out, he'll kill me. He's said so many times, and I know he will. I've seen him do it. He knows I want to leave, so he's added you and our parents to the threat. He'll kill you first if I escape, and then them."

He took several more steps, and I backed away until my body pressed against the wall behind me. A few more steps and he would be able to see into the room and know J was there. I prayed for help. Who was lying and who was telling the truth? How was I to know my enemies apart from my allies?

"I'm trapped, Jasmina, and I couldn't think of any way out." He took another step. "Not until Gar told me about this."

One more step, a glance, and Samir instantly had his knife in front of him again. "You!"

J stood still, like a tiger before the pounce, his knife gleaming in the rising sun. "I figured you'd come. Why bother lying to her?" He sent a quick glance my way. "Or is this all a ploy to get me to let you both go free?"

"I'm getting my sister out of here before Gar comes," Samir said, coming to the top of the stairs and standing in front of me. It was the first protective gesture I had ever seen him make.

"We will all wait here for Gar," J countered.

"Jasmina," Samir said, his voice no longer a boy's but a man's. "Go down the stairs. Now."

"What about Mother?" I whispered. "She's right next door."

"She isn't next door. Gar would never give us the real address. All of this was just to get you. But this time, he won't win."

I slumped to the ground, my back brushing the wall and setting free specs of dust to dance in the sunlight. "Where is she?" I asked. I couldn't take it anymore. All of this, for nothing?

"I heard Gar boast to one of his lackeys that he brought her back as a personal slave in his own house in the city, so he could always have something to hold over our heads. Accept it, Jasmina. There's no chance of setting her or our father free." He sent a quick look back to where I quivered on the floor. "Our only hope is to get out ourselves and get far away from Kolkata."

"You aren't taking her anywhere." J's voice was closer now, but I did not look up to see where he stood. I had curled into a ball behind Samir and hid my face. Away from Kolkata? Where could we go where Gar would not find us? And how could I ever leave knowing my parents would forever be prisoners to a man who enjoyed making others suffer? Even if we could escape, I would never be happy, knowing they would surely pay over and over again for our freedom.

Did I even believe Samir at all? After all he'd done, could this be another lie? But why would he lie about escape when just delivering me to Gar would be easier?

"God, who can I trust?" I lifted my face and whispered to the heavens.

"You can trust me." J stood near enough now that one swipe would slash his knife across Samir's skin.

"No, don't trust him. Trust me, Jasmina." Samir crouched, knees bent and arms out, ready to fight.

I wiped the tears from my face so I could see and made my choice. Let them fight up here in the dust. If my mother was not in this neighborhood, if I could not free her, I would not stay.

While knives swung through the air and my brother and my friend threatened each other, in one fluid motion I jumped up, grasped the railing, and ran.

thirty-one

Gar

I heard them shouting above me as I flew down the flight of stairs, slid across the dust covering the second floor, and ran down the large staircase toward freedom. I was swinging my body around toward the broken-glass window with thundering footsteps pounding above me as they ran after me, when I heard a loud click from behind. I stopped in my tracks, and I turned to see the knob of the front door spin.

As I stood immobile, the front door opened. He pushed his bulk through the door as if the house was his own, which it may have been—it would be like him to own a house that was luxuriously rich but filthy inside. He faced me, a gratified smile on his face.

"Hello, young one," Gar said. I had forgotten how even his voice could make me tremble. "I've been looking forward to seeing you again."

I heard J and Samir's steps halt at the top of the stairs but could not tear my gaze away from Gar's to see if either was surprised to see him. Gar glanced up and his smile widened.

"Ah, you are all here. How convenient. My men will be glad to not have to search to capture you."

Capture us all?

Gar took a step toward me, and I heard at least one set of footsteps coming down the stairs behind me. "I will look forward to returning to my home today, Jasmina, and telling your mother how I caught you, how you were captured trying to rescue her. This will cause her great suffering, don't you think?"

I had heard and seen and experienced enough. My anger was so fierce I was glad when Gar reached out and grabbed my wrist with his powerful, large hand. With a shout I yanked my arm free and loved the alarm on his face when I angled my body and lifted my leg, jamming my foot against the side of his fat-legged knee. He howled in pain and yelled for help.

Outside the door, some kind of struggle was taking place, for rather than coming in to help Gar, the men outside seemed to be having a battle of their own. I heard shouts but did not stop to be curious. I pivoted, searching for anything I could use as a weapon. If only those steel bars had been piled inside the window rather than out! I found a section of plank that had broken off that would fit in my hands and grabbed it, wincing as a splinter sliced into my palm.

Turning again, readying myself to attack, I instead stopped and stared. J was at the bottom of the stairs, standing over Gar, who had somehow ended up on the floor. J's large knife was aimed at Gar's neck. My brother stood near Gar's feet, his knife also out, but not toward J. Toward Gar.

For a moment, we all stared at each other, except for Gar who whined about his knee and kept yelling toward the front door for help.

"I thought you were on his side," J said to Samir.

"You're the one on his side," Samir responded.

"Neither of you are on his side," came a voice from the front. We all looked, even Gar, to see a solid, muscular man fill the doorway with his presence. For a split second, below his sunglasses, I saw his cheeks round out into a smile. "And it's a good thing, or I'd be arresting all of you with him."

He reached behind him and pulled out handcuffs, real ones, the first I had ever seen, and clamped them around Gar's struggling wrists. I was surprised they would fit.

"Ow! They're too tight!" Gar yelled.

I stared, silent and drowning in confusion, as if I'd been knocked over by a huge wave and could not tell which way was up. Mr. Sunglasses hefted Gar to his feet and escorted him toward the front door where he handed him over to another man also wearing sunglasses in the early morning light. Behind him, I could see several others all dressed the same, all pushing or directing Gar's lackeys toward waiting cars.

Mr. Sunglasses turned in the open doorway. "Good work, men," he said, and then even through the glasses I could tell he was looking at me. "Both of these men contacted me about Gar's plan to capture you, J by phone and Samir with a note he left at Amrita's salon. Thanks to them, we finally have the man at the top." He shouted a command out the door to the man shoving Gar into a car, and I shivered. His whole presence was intimidating and his shoulders so very large.

He started out the door but looked back once to say, "After we get him in jail, I'll be making a trip to his house to see if your mother really is there. I've already got a group at the brick kiln working to rescue your father." I nearly broke in two. He looked us over and his mouth turned upward. "For now I'll have one of my men drive you back to the compound to clean up and get some rest. I'll be in touch."

With that he was gone. The cars started, all but one, and drove away, and the curious neighbors who had gathered eventually wandered back to their homes. The house became as silent as it had been through the night.

I looked at J. At Samir. They looked at each other, and then at me. I wanted to hug them or question them or shout at them for putting me through such a fearful night and morning.

Unable to do any of those options, I promptly sat down right where I was and did the only thing I could do. I cried.

Safe Again

"No way! Then what happened?"

Milo dropped his crutch, he was so excited. He quickly sat next to Dapika and completed our circle on the large beige carpet in Grandmother's main visiting room. J, Samir, and I told our parts of the story with curious questions flying from Grandmother where she sat on her strange chair that rocked forward and back but never fell over, more questions about details from Mr. Mark who sat on the couch with baby Adiya, and no questions at all from Asha, who sat next to him with her eyes wide and full of tears.

We had arrived at the compound just after Asha and Mr. Mark had, and chaos ensued for a while. "We were worried and decided to come back right away this morning to see if Grandmother was any better," Asha had said, hugging me tight to her. "But when we got halfway here and received Dapika's message on the phone, I was terrified! You could have been captured, Jasmina!"

"Tell me about it," I said, using an English phrase Mr. Mark liked to say sometimes.

He grinned at me. "Whatever happened, I'm glad you're okay."

"What did happen?" Asha had asked, looking from me to Samir to J. "And who are these young men with you?"

I realized she had never seen either of them before. "This is my brother, Samir, and J, my friend." I still was not sure how much I trusted Samir, but sitting with him on the floor, watching the tension in him uncurl like a bedspring being stretched out straight, I started to feel hope.

When our story had ended, Mr. Mark gathered us together and prayed, speaking aloud the thanks I felt for God's rescue of us that morning. Samir, J, and I could all have been captured, but instead we were free, and Gar was finally caught.

When Mr. Mark's phone rang and it was the sunglasses man saying he was at Gar's house and yes, my mother was there, and my father was safe at a police station, I nearly unraveled completely. It was over. Five long years of slavery for them. Five long years of slavery or searching for me.

I could not let myself cry again, certainly not after I'd become such a dripping mess earlier at the house. I excused myself, claiming the need to clean up, which was a need indeed. Grandmother's carpet was already covered in a layer of dust from our clothing. Leaving the group behind, I made my way to Grandmother's guest room, the place I had called home for weeks, with the yellow blanket and soft bed and cheerful decorations. I chose a clean shalwar kameez and left it just outside the bathroom so it would not get wet as I poured dipper after dipper of cool, clean water over me, washing away the dirt and praying away the fear and anger and despair that had followed me for years and even now still clutched at my heart. I let God wash it all away, and when my bath and my prayers were complete, I felt new and whole again.

I would soon see my parents, not to deliver them from evil, but to welcome them to freedom.

"Thank You, God," I said in my empty room.

It was easy to express my gratitude to Him. It would not be quite as easy to express it aloud to Dapika, as I knew I needed to do.

I found her later with Milo on the compound orphanage steps. "Where are J and Samir?" I asked.

Milo stretched his bad leg out and rubbed his kneecap. "They're getting cleaned up inside." He grinned at me. "You look much better now that you're not covered in dirt. Your hair was as grey as Grandmother's."

"I'm glad you're okay," Dapika added, elbowing Milo, who elbowed her back with another grin. "I was really worried."

I nodded, knowing I needed to say it. If it hadn't been for her . . .

I told myself to be humble and tried to mold my mouth around the words Americans like to hear so much. Dapika was nearly American. She had lived on the compound for so long she would surely appreciate it, maybe even expect it.

"Dapika, I . . . I . . ." I nodded, which was supposed to go right before the word, but I still had trouble actually saying it. It felt so very un-Indian to use a word instead of a gesture or act. But no gesture or act would be adequate either.

Dapika's smile was knowing. "You're welcome," she said. "And just so you know, Grandmother hasn't taken any pills since last night. She's completely back to normal."

Relief. I nodded again and smiled. She understood. "I'd better get back," I said. "I know Asha wants to ask me more questions."

Turning to go, I heard Milo laugh behind me. "You're such an Indian."

I smiled as I crossed the compound. For some reason then, when it was just joking, I could say it. "Thanks," I threw back over my shoulder.

That made him laugh harder, and my smile widened. It was good to be back home.

thirty-three
Freedom

I had been walking with Asha while Mr. Mark got information from Samir when Mr. Sunglasses drove his car through the opened gate and parked it under an awning near the orphanage building.

Were my parents in that car? The back windows were tinted dark, and I could not tell. Sunglasses man stepped out. As I stood watching from a distance, I felt a soft hand on my shoulder and looked up to see Asha smiling at me. "You must be scared to death," she commented softly, and I appreciated that someone understood. I let my head tip to rest on her shoulder, unsure if I would ever be able to do so with my Indian mother. I had lived on the streets or with Americans for so many years, I found myself somewhat lost as to what would be acceptable within the culture of my own parents.

"I want to tell you a secret, Jasmina," Asha whispered as Mr. Sunglasses shut the driver's side door and walked over to talk with Mr. Mark. Samir approached to look in the tinted windows of the back seat of the car. So far no one else had emerged. "I'm going to have a baby."

My eyes lifted to see that hers were shining. She had wanted a baby for so long, but then they got little Adiya and now they would have another, perhaps a boy with hair like sunshine. I smiled and offered my congratulations, but wondered why she had chosen to tell me her news right then.

"I was going to wait to tell you," she said as if she knew my thoughts, "but I decided to tell you now so you would believe what I had to say."

I waited.

Her smile was full of love. One hand rested on her belly, while the other remained on my shoulder. "This child won't be born for many months yet, but even still, I know that I shall love this baby forever. It would not matter if we were separated for years or even a lifetime. I would never forget, and I would never stop loving my child. I am sure your mother feels the same way about you, Jasmina."

I nodded my thanks and, gulping down my hesitation, walked toward the car.

"It's empty," Samir said when I neared him. Those tinted windows suddenly felt like my heart; I could not see through the murky depths of my disappointment to know if any other feelings were inside.

"Your parents were rescued today," Mr. Sunglasses said, leaving Mr. Mark and coming to stand near. The murky swamp in my heart cleared and revealed a strange combination of fear and joy, unmixable, like oil and water.

"Please . . ." I could not form more words, was not even sure what I needed to know.

He leaned his body against the side of the car and crossed his big arms as he looked at me. "Do you really want to know?"

I wasn't sure, but I tilted my head in a quick gesture to the left side. Yes.

He nodded and spoke. "Your mother was locked in a small room in Gar's house." He waited, looking at me for some time before saying, "She was tied to a bedpost."

I gasped and fought tears.

"I learned that Gar kept her tied up at night, so she had to sleep that way, but over the past week he had been keeping her tied most of the day as well. He knew we were looking for her and probably did it to keep her from trying to reveal her presence to us if we arrived at his house and asked questions."

Samir joined us. "What about our father?" he asked.

"Wait, not yet," I said. "Please finish about Mother."

Samir went to stand beside Mr. Sunglasses, who continued talking. "We went there right after leaving you, with Gar in the car. I wanted him with me in case we needed his keys or needed him for recognition."

"Recognition?" I asked.

"For the slaves to say he was the one who trafficked them," Samir put in.

"We searched inside, leaving him guarded in the car, and found your mother and several others, all who said they were there by choice and did not want to leave."

"But that's not true!" I protested.

Samir looked at me like I was completely ignorant. He'd experienced such a transformation lately that it was almost a relief to see that familiar expression. "People will say anything if you beat them or threaten them enough," he said.

"We had papers of freedom to offer them, but no one would sign them," Sunglasses man continued with a shake of his head. I never thought about how frustrating his job must be sometimes. "So I had Gar brought in. They all started to run, but then I turned him around, and they saw the handcuffs. That changed everything. They stood and stared, not quite believing what they saw."

Mr. Mark joined us. I had never heard Sunglasses man speak so much. Maybe he usually told all of this to Amrita and was telling us because she was gone. Did he miss her as I did? More perhaps?

"I thought we had them, but they still wouldn't sign the papers or come with us out of the house. They were too afraid."

He stopped and stared across the compound until I could not keep silent. "What did you do?"

He surprised me by smiling. "I told your mother about you, how you escaped from slavery and had been searching for her, and that you were waiting for her. That did it. She marched right up and signed the papers first, and then gave a full testimony against Gar that we'll be able to use in court."

His smile widened. "Gar will be spending a very long time in jail."

Good News

I wanted to hug somebody, but none of the men standing with me were viable choices. Asha had gone inside. I wrapped my arms around myself and bounced on my heels. Mother was free!

"Thank You, God!" I said aloud.

"What about our father?" Samir asked again.

"Once we had Gar in custody, we called the team who had been waiting for word at the brick kiln. With that news they were able to rescue the slaves who had been sent to work there." He smiled again. "We originally thought it would just be your father, but when the team arrived, several other men asked for help. The team started asking questions and digging deeper, and they discovered multiple families of men, women, and children who had been sent there by Gar."

"All slaves?" I asked.

"All made to be slaves," he said. "They were forced to make bricks from sunrise to sunset, but were never paid."

"That is Gar's favorite method—other people doing all the work and him getting all the money," Samir said. I could tell he was angry; his fists were grabbing the sides of his shorts like he used to do when we were kids.

"Did you get our father out?" I asked Sunglasses man.

"We did. And one hundred and twelve others." I had never seen him smile so much. A happy feeling started in my heart and spread. "And this is just the beginning. With Gar in jail, we'll be able to free people he enslaved all over this city."

That happy feeling inside ballooned until I thought it might burst out of me. "Can I see my mother?"

His look on me was kind, which is why I was surprised when he shook his head no. "I did not bring them directly here. We give newly rescued victims some time before reuniting them with family or friends. Sometimes they need medical attention or just a few days to process what happened and realize they are now free." He nudged his glasses up his nose. "And there is a mountain of paperwork that must be done as well."

I noticed he avoided saying if our parents in particular needed medical help, and I accepted the secrecy. Sometimes information hurt more than it helped. I would pray for them both, for whether they had wounds needing a doctor's attention or not, it was certain they had wounds—visible or invisible—that needed God's.

"Where are they?" I had to put my head back to look up at him. He should marry a tall woman, else his wife would live with a sore neck. Amrita had been tall. The thought filled me with a sudden sadness. How was it possible to be both happy and sad at the same time?

"We took them to the House of Hope. It is outside the city and quieter. For some, freedom after so long in slavery is a difficult adjustment. The House of Hope is run by people who care and will help your father and mother in whatever way they need."

I turned to my brother. "I've heard of the House of Hope many times. It is a good place. That's where they took J's sister after she was rescued. Now she's . . . I don't know where she is."

My head tilted to look at Mr. Sunglasses again. "When will we get to see our parents?"

"I will come when it is time."

"You are staying there?" I had never heard of him or any of the other international liaisons staying there.

"For now." He turned to wave at Mr. Mark. "I must go. There is work for me to do in the city tonight."

Would he go to Amrita's salon and look for clues? I wanted to tell him about the secret passageway, but surely he knew of it.

He drove away, and Samir looked at me. "How can you want to see them?" he asked, genuine confusion in his voice. "They have suffered enough for what they did, so I'm glad they are free, especially Mother. But I can't face them yet." He stepped closer. "I still want to hate them, but you don't. How do you keep from hating them?"

We walked, and I told my brother about Amrita and how hate fueled her heart and her actions, and how in the end she was more imprisoned by hate than she had ever been by any trafficker. I told him about Dapika and how her ever-present fear changed, how she changed when she gave her life to Jesus. I told him how I had found the freedom from hating him and our parents by letting Jesus have my heart and make it new.

He listened, this brother of mine who used to sell others. "You do have reason to hate me," he said, his brows down and pensive. "As much as we both have reason to hate our father."

"But I will not. I feel like I want to sometimes, but I will not let hate have me, just as I would not let a trafficker have me if I ever had the choice." I stopped walking and faced him. "Neither of us had the choice when we were sold, but we both have the choice now whether we will be truly free or not."

"What if he hasn't changed? What if he treats you like I did . . . or worse?"

I sighed. "He may. But even if he does, I will not let him, or anyone else, destroy me."

Samir had his hands in his pockets as we started walking again. The sun had just set, and I could barely see him in the encroaching darkness. "You really are free, aren't you?"

Stars began to twinkle above us cheerfully. "Yes." I looked up. "I belong to the one who made the stars and knows them all by name." With a smile, I moved forward. "Walk with me awhile, and I'll tell you more about Him."

Danger

Mr. Sunglasses drove into the compound every day the rest of that week. The first day he spent shut up in the guest house with Samir, where he offered my brother a deal he gladly and gratefully took. Samir exchanged all the information he knew about Gar's trafficking business and who shot Amrita, and he promised to testify in the trials against Fayeed and Gar, in exchange for not having to go to jail himself. He even told the sunglasses man about the quarry owner and his connection to Gar, something Mr. Sunglasses did not know about.

The second day the large car made its way through the compound gate again, and that day Mr. Sunglasses spent with J, likely getting all the information he could from him and checking it with Samir's to see if they matched. As sincere as my brother seemed to be now, I would still want to check his facts, though I was inclined to believe him and even feel a little proud of how much he was helping shut down the very system he had once wallowed in.

By the third day, when Sunglasses man still did not talk with me but rather spent his time with Mr. Mark, I decided to try to stay busy, helping Asha with the baby and spending time with Grandmother, who was back to her delightful self again. Still the day trudged by, like when I used to try to run fast alongside the ocean but the wet sands sucked my feet down with each step.

Finally, the fourth day, he summoned me. I went willingly, quick to ask about my parents and when I would be able to see them.

"It might be sooner than I'd planned," he said to my surprise. I smiled but he did not smile back. "Sit down, Jasmina."

Curious, I lowered my body into a chair near him. We were in the largest room of the guest house, a space empty except for neat rows of chairs all facing one direction, as if set up for a meeting. He twisted his chair to face me. "I have heard from both Samir and J that your face is known in the city."

I nodded, my questions silenced by the sudden apprehension that floated around me.

"Samir must not remain here. Nor should J." He adjusted his sunglasses, not even removing them for our private meeting. I wondered if he wore them in his sleep. "My connections in the city inform me that we have created mayhem here in this section of Kolkata. Gar supplied children and adults to smaller trafficking businesses all over the city, and now with him in jail, a lot of people who worked under Gar or worked alongside Gar are angry. Since Gar of course did not share his secrets as to how he obtained his supply of victims, traffickers all over the city are finding themselves with no new slaves to sell. They are losing a vast amount of money every day."

"That's wonderful," I offered.

"It is," he agreed, "but dangerous for anyone who was involved in putting Gar away. The more business the traffickers lose, the more dangerous it is. They are on the lookout."

"For Samir?" I asked, biting my lip. "To get revenge?"

"Some want information more valuable than revenge. Samir knows where the victims came from. Whoever could get that information would have acccss to Gar's position and power." A tremor ran through me, but then the man smiled. "That's why I'm inclined to believe your brother truly does want out of the system for good. He could be one of the most powerful traffickers in the city if he wanted. Instead he has been telling us Gar's secret information, and with it we will be able to shut down many of the sources that have been feeding our city's slave trade."

"Where will you take him?" I decided that later I would try to wrap my mind around this new idea of my brother being honorable, but for now would get the facts. "Will you take J as well?"

"We will go to the House of Hope. J's sister and her friend were moved to another safe location outside the city, so there is room."

My hands clenched. "The House of Hope? Where my parents are?"

He nodded. "And you will come as well."

I was standing before I realized it. "When?"

"Next week. From what they tell me, if the traffickers in the city know your connection to Amrita and your relation to Samir, you are in as much danger as either of them. If someone were to find your location, it would be dangerous for all of you as well as the others who live here."

The tremor that had run down my back now raced back up. I suddenly remembered the boy I had seen in a tree outside the compound, watching us. At the time, I had assumed he was a bored street kid and had not paid him much attention, but now the fact that he had scurried out of sight the moment I noticed him seemed cause for concern. I told Mr. Sunglasses and his face went grave.

"Next week is too late then," he said. "I had hoped for more time for your parents to adjust and for me to finish my work here in the city." He stood and turned his chair back in line with the others. "But I, too, have become recognizable here and must hand the work over to others. Life will change for all of us." He looked at me, and I wished I could see his eyes. "Let us pray to the God we both serve that it will be for the good."

After a few basic instructions, he left the building to go once more into the city, and I left the building to go tell everyone that J, Samir, and I would be leaving in the morning, uncertain of when or if we would return.

thirty-six
My Mother

The goodbyes had been hard. I told myself Milo and Dapika would be just fine without me. They had each other. Asha and Mr. Mark and the baby were a complete family. I would miss them terribly, but I could never endanger them by remaining. Grandmother had been the hardest to leave. She had hugged me tight and told me to always remember that God loved me more than even she did, and He had a great plan for my life.

I rested my feet up on my one bag of possessions and distracted my melancholy thoughts by wondering what that plan might be. In a way it was good that the separation had to happen quickly. Once Samir and I were reunited with my parents, we would be a family again. Would Samir submit to their authority? I knew I should, for God's book said we were to honor and obey our parents. What if my father only wanted to marry me off to some ancient rich man so Father could live comfortably off the dowry money, or what if he decided to sell us again?

God did have a plan, I told myself. I hoped His plan did not include marriage to an ancient man, rich or not.

Like a wave clutching at the shore, the one worry that kept coming was the thought of returning to life as it had been before. What if we all went back to the sea, to a one-room bamboo hut, surrounded by the vast ocean on one side and on the other side a village of people who knew nothing beyond the extent of their own eyesight? Could I be content in such a life again, where my physical being had no room for privacy and my mind was allowed no room for dreams? Mother always said that large desire was endless poverty. Would I have to choose poverty of the body and poverty of the spirit?

Perhaps it was God's plan for me to show His love to my parents by serving them, unselfishly setting aside my own desire to learn and my passion to make a difference, and yes, my hope for friends and maybe someday even love, and live only wanting to make their lives better.

That idea was enough to keep me in silent prayer the rest of the drive, long as it was. Samir in the backseat beside me and J in the front both talked with Mr. Sunglasses about who would replace him and if they could get jobs like his. Their voices were filled with awe, and understandable as it was, I wanted to remind Samir that soon our lives and our choices would no longer be our own. He would not agree though. I knew he would say our father forfeited the right to decide our fates when he sold us.

Was he right? How was I to think and how was it possible to have an argument with so many different perspectives going on in just my own one mind? I rubbed my temples and fought the nausea that rose with every curve of the country roads.

When we stopped, my relief was great right up until I stepped from the car and saw the sign hanging on a green metal gate. We had arrived at the House of Hope. My nausea was gone, but in its place sat a heavy weight, like someone had dropped a stone into my stomach. I held both hands to my middle. What would my parents think when they saw me? What would I think when I saw them?

J exited the car and stood at my side. We had not spoken much since the abandoned house, always surrounded by so many others, like Milo who had plenty to say and left little room for deeper conversation.

"You will see your parents today," he said, looking forward toward the two mud homes and a wooden building—a chicken coop?—set back a distance behind them. Fields of varying crops ripened in the sun around the buildings, and I also saw flowers, testament that beauty was valued here as well as resourcefulness. Something about the place felt safe. "Are you scared?"

"Yes," I admitted, wanting to pretend I was not, yet not wanting to pretend with him. I glanced to see he was now looking at me, and his eyes were kind.

"I can imagine," he said, and I remembered that he was an orphan, left on the doorstep of an orphanage in a basket with his sister. I thought of how he would probably give anything to know his parents. I thought of Dapika and how she would give anything to have her mother safe with her again. Their lack reminded me what a gift it was to have parents at all, and I took courage.

Samir and Mr. Sunglasses had gone ahead into one of the buildings. I stood still and J remained beside me. I was waiting for my stomach to stop clenching so I would not stagger when I walked.

"I'll be here if you need . . ."

He left his sentence unfinished, and I wondered what words he might have said. I smiled. "This place doesn't seem dangerous," I said, putting my hands to my hips. "I don't think I'll need you to rescue me by holding a knife to my throat for the third time."

He chuckled. "It's a good thing. My knife is still back at that mansion where I dropped it." He sobered, and his voice went low. "I hope to never need it again."

My smile spread. "Then what help could I possibly need from you?" I was itching to go inside, yet also reluctant, so

I chose to stay to hear J's response. He did not answer, only smiled at me, and as I looked at his face I realized what he was offering me. Not a rescue in a dangerous situation, but help for the situation I now faced. His friendship in case meeting my parents was not all I hoped it to be.

He was telling me I was not alone, and I hoped my eyes expressed the gratitude I could not say, for right at that moment a woman emerged from the mud home, her long dark hair braided and the braid in a knot behind her head, her sari worn but clean, her skin dark like mine, her eyes shining with tears.

My mother.

At once I knew her, though she was thinner and aged, and I felt a sob rise in my throat. She gasped. "Jasmina," she breathed out. "My baby girl."

With my hands still on my stomach, I walked toward the woman who had taught me to read and told me secret tales of adventure and filled me with a curiosity about the world beyond our one-room hut. As I neared her, I imagined I could smell the sea air in her hair and that we could go walk along the shore once the chores were done, talking of the dreams she had once had for herself and had transferred to me.

My legs bent and I reached low to touch the tops of her feet and then my own head, a show of honor that for the first time in my life felt insufficient. I wanted to hug her. She rested a hand on my head, a blessing, and I heard her crying. She had not forgotten me.

"Jasmina." I stood at Mr. Sunglasses' voice and saw him gesture to his right. "There is a nice garden behind the house," he said. "You could take your mother, and she could show you the flowers if you'd like."

He was offering me privacy, a moment away from all the eyes and ears I suddenly noticed were in every open window of the mud building. Again, I hoped my eyes communicated gratitude as I walked with my mother—*my mother*, I still could barely believe it—away from the others to ask what her life had been like these years. How had they survived? What would happen now? I had so many questions and yet found myself walking silently beside her, not needing to talk, content just to be with her and know that all this time, through all the years and all my longings, I had been loved.

We sat at the back edge of the field, and it was then my mother spoke. She told me of her loneliness after we were taken and my father's shame. She shared how they were deceived into slavery, how Gar took them into the city to the huge house, and how hopeful they were at finally having easy jobs. How much it shamed my father when the job turned into domestic slavery and the certainty that it meant Samir and I had been made slaves too. She told me how my father suffered in silence and, though he would never speak of it openly, how she knew he was sorry for what he had done and would never be free of it.

I thought of Amrita saying she would never be free of her hate. People could be bound by so many things, I realized. Fear, hate, shame, unfulfilled longings. I chose right then not to let anything but God have me, ever, not even disappointment if my dreams had to be set aside. I would not live enslaved ever again.

When my mother's memories reached the present, she asked for mine, but I asked questions until the sun began to set. As we walked back to the mud dwelling, I handed her the diary I had kept in my hands since we had left the compound, the notebook I had filled with words for her. I wanted her to know my story—all of it, the good and the bad—before we talked again. Some things within it I felt I could not say.

She took it from me and ran her hand gently across the cover, as if it were a treasure embossed in gold, rather than a once thrown-away notebook with burned edges. Her hand lifted to my hair again. "Look at you, my daughter," she said, her voice as gentle as I remembered. "So many nights I begged all the gods to protect you. I feared you were suffering, mistreated, even dead. And now I see you are a beautiful young woman, educated and smart, and free. I will thank the gods tonight." She smiled. "No, you are a follower of the Jesus God, the God who loves people. I will thank Him."

I stared in silent wonder as she led me into the building and brought me to my father, who seemed so much smaller than I remembered. With stooped shoulders and eyes downcast, he greeted me and also put his hand over my hair in blessing, but then walked into a room and shut the door. Had my mother not informed me, I would have taken his actions for rejection rather than seeing in them his shame. Had he done the same to Samir? Had they spoken at all yet?

Mother led me to the room that was to be my own for a time. After she said goodnight I sat on the small bed, not unzipping the bag which someone, likely J, had kindly brought inside for me. Mother had talked about my faith in Jesus, but I had not told her any of my story yet. How had she known?

I wanted to leave my room and find her and ask. However, the fatigue I had seen on her face kept me seated on the bed, thinking over the mystery until I finally put my bag on the floor and lay down to rest my head on the pillow. There, as I puzzled, sleep found and claimed me until the morning.

thirty-seven
The Letter

My first day at the House of Hope was one of hope indeed. Samir surprised me by following our mother everywhere she went, like a newborn lamb would, basking in her every attention. Mother led us around the property, telling us how the House of Hope came to be and about the victims who had found a place of refuge there. She introduced us to Rashid, the proprietor, and his wife, Neena, who had been burned by acid, and though half of her face was distorted, she smiled with such joy it was impossible to feel sorry for her. Their three children ran through the fields and chased the chickens, and their laughter was medicine to the heart and soul. We continued our tour and Mother introduced us to other rescued victims, but she did not take us to the second mud home, saying we could go there the following day.

When my father summoned Samir and all the others had gone back to their work in the fields, my mother took my hand and smiled down on me. The sunshine was bright, and instead of the coarse sounds of the city I heard birds chirping and the children singing a happy tune.

"I stayed up late last night reading your diary, Jasmina," she said, and the smile I had been wearing fell. I had been certain she had not read it yet, not when she greeted me so lovingly that morning. Now she knew my secrets and my sins. I lowered my head.

"I'm so glad you gave it to me to read." She lifted my chin with her hand. "I feel I know you now." Her eyes filled with tears. "You did suffer, as I feared. How I wish I could take those years back. I wish I had done something to stop him from taking you and your brother away. I have lived with such regret for so long."

"You couldn't have stopped it," I said, and in my statement somehow I set myself free from the same regret. "And even if we could have, it is in the past. We are free now."

"Yes. And you were so brave, and I am so proud." She turned my hand palm up. "And your handwriting is quite nice too."

I laughed. "I had a good teacher." As much as I wanted to say something to keep her smiling, the question pressed upon me and begged for release. "Mother, what will happen now? With you and Father . . . and me and Samir?"

She sighed, and we walked in silence together, hand in hand, for a while until she spoke. "Your father does not wish to remain here. The people offered him a job, but everything here reminds him of his failure, his shame. When the papers are finished, we will return to the sea. He will be a fisherman again, his own boss."

I gulped, feeling my life narrow to one room of bamboo, a dirt floor, open windows letting in bugs, the smell of fish permeating my clothes and hunger gnawing at my stomach. "And Samir? And me?" I asked.

"Were there a simple choice, you would return with us—Samir to learn to take over the fishing business and care for us in our old age, you to a marriage and new life with your husband's family."

Both of my lips were clamped between my teeth to keep my protests inside. I would let God do His will. I would let His plan for me prevail. Even if it meant the death of every dream I had.

She squeezed my hand. "Fortunately for you, and I am truly glad, for I do not wish on you the life that I have lived, the simple choice is not available any longer."

My face shot up and I looked her in the eye. "What? Why?"

Her slim hand reached into the folds of her sari. I cocked my head, looking at the white envelope she brought out. It had no writing on it, no marks of any kind. "What is it?"

She handed it to me. "It is for you." I started to open it but she stopped my hands. "Go to your room. You will want to read it alone. It is from a friend."

For some reason, I thought of how my mother knew I was a follower of Jesus, and how several other things she had mentioned that day revealed she knew more about me than I had shared with her. Who was this friend who had been talking with her about me? Had Asha called the House of Hope before we came? Or Grandmother?

Once inside my room, I lifted the flap and pulled out a sheet of paper. Unfolding it, my eyes dropped until I found the signature at the bottom. When I saw it, my hands shook, and the paper fluttered to the ground. I followed, landing on the floor, my gaze fastened on the paper and the name on it.

The letter was from Amrita.

thirty-eight

Amrita

Dear Jasmina,

As you may have guessed by the presence of this letter, I am not dead. Forgive me for not letting you know sooner, but I was unconscious for many days and only recently have been strong enough to speak or write. During the blur of days and nights when I neared the clutch of death and the terror of judgment beyond it, I learned something very important: as awful as a life of hatred was, to die carrying nothing but hatred and bondage with me was worse in a way I never want to experience again.

Jasmina, I am where you are, here at the House of Hope. Our international friend brought me here the night I was shot. I am staying in the mud home next to where you are with a woman named Neena, who is filled with such joy she shines. I knew her before but never saw her radiance because my eyes were always distracted by the distortion of her acid-burned face.

She does not hide her scars and disfigurement as I hide mine. As the days have passed, and I have watched her peace, I see a freedom in her that I long for. I am going to chase it. Today I took off one of my bangles. I know, it is not much. In fact, the loss of it does not reveal even the edge of my scars. But I am not one accustomed to change. If I have the courage, I shall remove another one tomorrow, and another the day following. I calculated that if I remove one each day, it shall take over three weeks before I am rid of them, but Neena says that love is patient.

Love. It is a word I have not known in any sense other than how it is spelled and how it sounds coming through the mouth. Hate has been the thread connecting me to others all my life. I thought it kept me safe, but it kept me a slave. The madam did not mind my hate for her. She feasted on it, for it kept me her prisoner, chained forever to my need to make her suffer for how she had hurt me.

With the bangles, with each one removed, I am giving a piece of myself to Jesus. I know you must be surprised, Jasmina, but truly I have longed to be His for so long, and it is only my foolish pride and my need for revenge that kept me from admitting it. Neena says His love is greater than anyone's, so that would mean His love is the most patient. I'm asking Him to wait for me, to help me tear off the layers of bitterness that still hold me tight. I want to believe there is something about me more valuable than the beauty of my face and body. I want to know what love is, how to accept it, and how to return it. I want to be free.

Jasmina, I am glad I was shot. I am glad the God who knows us both knew what path I was leading you down and where it would end. He protected you from my fate, and I now know He was sparing me my own deserved fate as well. He has given me another chance. I suppose I already know His love is patient. Neena says there are more words that describe Jesus, words like truth and peace and kindness and gentleness. To think of God as gentle is something beyond my comprehension. I have never been treated with gentleness in my life, not until here by Neena and by my international friend. Asha tried to, and I remember others who tried, but I turned them away.

There is much we need to discuss, Jasmina, but my hand hurts, and my body is weak. I must stop writing for now. After you read this, come to the mud home next door. Hopefully I will be awake and we can talk in person. I must warn you though, you will find me much changed.

Your friend,
Amrita

I folded the letter and sat staring at the wall, my thoughts like shells rolling onto the seashore, settling on the sand only to be picked up and tossed by the waves again and again. Amrita was alive. I was not guilty of the death of a friend. She was much changed, she said. She meant a change in appearance, but I could already read the change on the inside of her. I should go and talk with her immediately.

But I found I could not. I had not realized the burden my guilt over her death had placed upon my shoulders. As I tried to rise from the floor, my legs buckled under me. I caught myself by clinging to the bed at my side, and then just gave in and threw myself on the bed to sob out the release of my fears for Amrita's eternity without Jesus and my pain at the loss of my friend and the aching weight of my fault in her death. I had cried more since her death than my entire previous existence.

After my tears were spent I must have slept, for when I sat up and looked through the window of my room, I saw the sun had traveled to the other side of the sky. It was not yet dark but would be soon. Had she been waiting for me?

I rushed from the room, using my orna to wipe my face and using my hands to tame down my hair. Outside the door of the first mud home, I found Mr. Sunglasses standing beside his car, talking with both J and Samir. When he saw me, he smiled, said something to the guys, and then walked toward me.

"Thank you for giving Amrita some time to rest after writing that note," he said, kindly saving me embarrassment. "She is awake now. I will take you to her."

I followed him into the other dwelling and soon found myself in a room looking down where Amrita lay propped up in bed, her long black hair fanning out along the pillow and spilling over her shoulders. She was pale, void of makeup, and somehow more beautiful than ever.

"Amrita," I said, my throat clogging up with emotion. "I'm so glad you're alive."

"So am I." She gave a small, weak laugh. "And we can talk all about that later, but for now, I have two important things to tell you." She reached up her hand, and Mr. Sunglasses took it in both of his. "The first is that this man and I are married." She smiled at my gasp. "He married me yesterday—me like this, without even any makeup on. Can you imagine?"

I was stunned at the joy on her face. "I'm so happy for you," I said.

"When I was young," Amrita continued, shifting on the bed to sit up more. "I dared to dream of being married someday, of having my own daughter." She frowned. "The things the madam forced me to do destroyed my body and all my hopes of having a child. And yet I find God can replace even dead, broken things of the past. Here I am, me, being loved. And I may even, in a way, get a daughter as well."

The sunglasses man, Amrita's new husband, pulled the covers higher on Amrita and smiled at her. "How about I tell her and you rest a bit?" She nodded, and he turned his smile to me. "Now that Amrita is well enough to travel, we will be leaving tomorrow morning. We are going to a place I will not name yet, far away, where another group like mine works to fight human trafficking and rescue the helpless. There is an international school there and an orphanage."

"J has already agreed to go," Amrita added. "His sister and her friend are already there."

"Samir will go as well." The man must have seen the questions in my eyes, for he continued. "We talked with your parents yesterday and explained the danger you both are in. They agreed with us that either of you moving with them back to your former home would not be safe."

My mouth dropped open but I had no words to say. It was fortunate there was a chair behind me, else I might have fallen to the floor. I sat most ungracefully.

"For you, Jasmina, you could remain here for a time, and possibly then go live safely with your parents," Amrita said, "though I don't like the idea. If you could stay with them, that would be one thing, but you know it would not last. Your mother told me you'd have a marriage arranged right away and would have to move anyway. However, we wanted to leave the choice to you."

"To me?" I had feared having no say in my future at all, and now the biggest choice of my life was handed right to me. I had no idea what to do with it.

"You won't have much time to decide," Amrita continued. "But we would like you to come with us. You are smart and brave and exactly what I would have wanted a daughter to be. Pearls are of no value in a desert, and your gifts would be wasted cooking all day in a bamboo hut for some new husband's mother."

"That's a nice proverb," the sunglasses man said.

"Jasmina likes proverbs."

He grinned. "I only know one proverb. To control the mind is like trying to control a drunken monkey that has been bitten by a scorpion."

"That's the only one you know?" Amrita sighed, but smiled. "Jasmina, we shall have to educate him."

We talked a bit longer but my mind was so clouded I could not recollect anything we said. I left the one building and returned to the other, finding my room and kneeling by my bed to ask God what I should do. Later I found my mother and father, and we talked about it. I even asked Samir his opinion.

J was the final person to ask. I found him outside just after dinner. "Have you decided yet?" he asked.

"No." I bit my lip. "What do you think I should do?"

He shrugged and smiled. "I'm not a good person to ask."

"Why not?" I felt my nose crinkle up as I squinted against the setting sun behind him. "You're my friend. You said if I needed you . . ."

"I am your friend." He was looking at me, but I could not see his eyes, only his silhouette with the light behind him. "But my reasons for wanting you to come with us would be selfish ones."

At that I wished I was the one silhouetted so he could not see the blush creeping across my cheeks. "Oh," I said, and turned to go inside.

He walked alongside me. "I can't tell you what you should do, but I can pray for you."

"I wish you would," I said, hoping my cheeks were back to their normal color. "I need some help."

"God is a good one to ask for that." He smiled at me before going inside. "See you tomorrow, Jasmina."

I stood outside, alone, staring at the car Mr. Sunglasses would drive away tomorrow, asking God if I should be in it or not. I prayed until the night mastered the day, and then remained awhile longer, looking up at the stars that all had names, knowing that the God who made them and named them would always be with me, no matter where I was.

thirty-nine
The Choice

My bag was packed. I spent some of the morning writing a note of love and farewell to Asha and Grandmother, and another note to Dapika and Milo. The rest of the morning I spent with my mother, trying to fit years of missed conversations into an hour or so.

"We will write letters," my mother said, as we walked to the waiting car. Mr. Sunglasses was gently carrying Amrita from the mud home. We stepped back to give them room. "I will find a way to mail letters to you. Being able to talk through mail will be much better than the past years of silence."

"I will write you often, Mother," I said. "And I don't want you to be lonely. There is a girl named Dapika at the missionary compound. She misses her mother and I know she would like to see the ocean. Could I suggest she come visit you sometime?"

"Of course." My mother beamed, though I could not tell if her happiness was over the thought of someone coming to visit or my care for her in suggesting it. She pulled me close. "I love you, Jasmina, and I'm so proud of you."

"I love you, too, Mother." I blinked, determined not to cry. Not today. "I'm so glad you're free."

"We are all free now," she said. "Your God has been very kind to us."

"I hope He will be your God one day too."

Her smile was like the sunshine rising. "He just might."

Amrita called to me from the backseat of the car. "You can be back here with me, Jasmina, and the men can sit up front."

I said goodbye to my father, who I noticed stood a little taller that morning. Samir shook his hand like a man, and I believe there was forgiveness in it. What a freeing force forgiveness was.

This was it. It was time to go and face the future. I did not know where we were going or even if we would remain in India. So many unknowns, and yet I did not feel afraid. I was God's child. He would guide me every step.

Bits of excitement seemed to burst and glow within me, like stars in the night sky. I watched as Samir threw his bag into the open trunk. He climbed in the car to sit in the middle of the front seat. J put his backpack into the trunk, and then came over to get my bag. "I'm glad you're coming with us," he said, and I felt my cheeks burn again. He chuckled and walked to the car, getting in and shutting the passenger door.

Mr. Sunglasses shook hands all around. We walked to the car together, where I was shocked speechless to see him lift his glasses and wink at his new wife. "Ready, my love?"

She grimaced as she scooted over for me, but then smiled. "Ready, Husband."

I turned from where I stood at the door and looked one last time at my parents, but not with too much sadness, for I felt sure I would see them again one day. I called out one last goodbye, and then I slipped into the car and shut the door.

"I'm ready, too. Let's go."